FIRE BREATHING ARMAND

Dragons of the Bayou

CANDACE AYERS

Lovestruck Romance Publishing, LLC

When Armand meets Angel, he knows she's not his mate.
She can't be—she's pregnant with another male's child.
Yet, no female has ever claimed his heart as she has.

Angel of Death is cursed.
Everyone around her dies.
The trick, she's learned, is to never get close to anyone.
Damned if she hasn't screwed that up, and her screwup may endanger the lives
of the two people she cares for the most—the man she's trying desperately not to
fall in love with, and her own newborn daughter.

Armand is willing to give up eternal life to spend what little time he has left
with Angel.
The only problem is, if he dies, Angel will take the blame.

Chapter One
ANGEL

I was starving. No exaggeration. My stomach was gnawing away at itself like a bottomless pit with teeth. Lately, my body was demanding that I eat everything in sight just to temporarily stave off raging hunger pangs. Problem was, there was currently no food in sight.

My legs moved as fast as pregnantly possible in search of sustenance—so, not very fast. I craved food more than I wanted to take off the tight bra that was binding my swollen breasts.

The streets of New Orleans were teaming with people as I weaved and waddled my way through the crowds while absently rubbing the protrusion at my middle. The exertion of walking from the church to the cemetery and back had burned off all my breakfast and I was beyond due for my midmorning meal.

A cloud of melancholy hung over me like a matching accessory to my black funeral dress. I wish I'd gotten to know Amie and Jeremiah better before their untimely demises. We'd planned on spending more quality time getting to know one another, but every time we got together, the conversation naturally turned to the pregnancy, prenatal care, plans for the delivery, and things along that line. I would always regret not learning more about them while they were alive. Who would have thought our time for that would be limited?

Fear about the future overwhelmed me, as it had so often in the past few days. The baby wiggled and became more active as I wallowed in my guilt and confusion. It was like the baby knew.

Maybe she was chastising me.

Maybe she blamed me?

Well, her motives aside, she was tap dancing on my bladder. She gave it a couple of good, strong kicks that nearly knocked the pee right outta me. I looked around for the nearest public restroom. Nothing. I considered making an effort to search for one while I was still able to hold it, but right about then, a delicious scent wafted through the air.

Stomach rumbling, I followed the aroma around the corner and spotted the source a block or so down—a food truck.

Clotilde's Cajun Crepes was parked perfectly along the street, drawing a crowd that formed a long line down the block. My bladder was nearing critical mass and I knew I was chancing it by getting food first, but my hands were shaky and I felt like I was going to pass out. So, I crossed my fingers that the crepe servers were working at top speed today, and I got in line behind a group of teenagers.

That might have been the wrong decision. A few minutes later, I found myself plastering my thighs together while I prayed for the ability to hold my pee just long enough to collect my crepe and waddle off to the nearest ladies' room. I was eight and a half months pregnant, though, so it was a crap shoot. Sucking my lip between my teeth, I leaned out of the line to see how far I was from the front. Still at least ten people ahead of me, but there were already another five or six people behind me. If I didn't stay where I was, I'd lose my place in line and, who knew, maybe end up fainting from starvation.

"You take one step out of line, lady, don't think you're getting back in."

Rude. I glared at the crass man behind me. He was about in his midforties, with dark, beady little eyes, a round, squashy build, and thinning hair. Definitely old enough to know good manners, especially when dealing with a pregnant woman. I wanted to ask him how come his momma didn't teach him any, but it came out differently. "Excuse me? What the fuck are you, the line police?"

He shrugged. "I'm just saying. We're all hungry."

Our verbal exchange had attracted the attention of the teenagers in front of me and several of them were openly staring—at me. WTH? There were a few whispers and giggles.

I told myself to stay calm but whispers and giggles had become triggers for me in the last couple of years. I could feel my face burning red and wanted to throat punch No-Manners, who'd started it. "I'm just standing here. Mind your business."

"Yeah, whatever. I'm warning you is all. Don't think you can use that condition of yours as an excuse for special treatment. You're no hungrier than the rest of us."

I tilted my head and contemplated the idea of faking full-blown labor pains. Maybe that would teach the ill-mannered asshat not to harass a pregnant woman. I had to pee so bad, though, I wasn't sure I could do a decent fake-job. "Just...stop talking to me."

More giggles and then a young, attractive blonde looked up from her phone and gasped. "It's her! It's that Angel of Death lady!"

I balled my hands into fists, nails digging into my palms, and stared down at my black flats, sensible shoes for a funeral. My heart pounded and my pulse raced. I felt the blood rushing to my face and heating my cheeks.

Remain calm. Remain calm.

Maybe if I ignored them, they'd go away. I remembered a trick I'd read about in a self-help book. To maintain one's serenity, one must trick the mind into thinking it was elsewhere. I hurriedly visualized myself lying on a beach in the Caribbean, skiing in the Swiss Alps, on a safari deep in the Congo—no go. My mind knew right where reality was located.

"No shit. Didn't she kill like a handful of people?"

"A dozen, I think. She cursed them is what it was."

"No, idiot. She's just like...really bad mojo."

"I wouldn't even stand that close to her, if I were you. Some of that bad mojo could get on you!"

I was instantly aware of the breathing room I was afforded as space opened around me and the crowd backed off.

Remain calm. Remain calm.

I closed my eyes for a second, then lifted my chin, moved forward in line, and pretended nothing out of the ordinary was happening. Seven people between me and the food truck. Seven. I could do it. Damn the south and it's superstitions.

"Dark-voodoo Lady, stay away from me!" The boy who'd asked if I'd killed people was obviously terrified of my curse, or my mojo, rubbing off on him. His raised voice drew even more attention, and I could see people holding up their phones to capture the moment for posterity. Or social media. "Don't let her touch you; her hocus-pocus is deadly."

The teenagers giggled and shrieked like they were kindergarteners playing a game of cooties, while the guy behind me grumbled about how I probably thought I deserved special treatment because of my celebrity status. Yeah, sure, being dubbed Angel of Death by the media certainly was something I wanted to capitalize on. By all means, allow me use the hideous moniker to gain favors.

All I really wanted, of course, was to be left alone and not bullied by a group of teenagers. Was that special treatment? More people stared.

I tried to step out of line, but I bumped into someone walking by.

"Watch out! O-M-G, you got some on you!" One of the teenage girls squealed, laughing like it was the funniest thing in the world.

The woman I'd bumped into gave me the stink eye and hurried away. The man behind me closed the gap I'd left in line and leveled me a haughty look, daring me to argue.

"I warned you," he snickered. "You can go to the end of the line now."

Baby Girl kicked and did some acrobatic move inside, putting more pressure on my bladder, and before I could stop it, a trickle of warm liquid flooded my panties and ran down my legs.

Of course, they noticed.

"Oh my god! She just pissed herself!"

"Eww, gross."

The tears I'd been holding back for days threatened to break loose, and all I could do was turn and run as fast as my overburdened body could take me before I further embarrassed myself by adding "blubbering crybaby" to their lists of my offenses.

My feet played Slip'n Slide in my wet flats as I waddled off at top speed. Crepes be damned.

Chapter Two

ANGEL

"Hellooo! Hellooo, there! Angel, right?"

Panting hard, I stopped to lean against the side of a brick building to catch my breath. I hadn't made it very far from the delinquent hyenas' giggles and cackles, but I was far enough that I could no longer hear their catcalls.

A woman from the funeral had followed me, and it appeared she was trying to get my attention. I recognized her. Her name was Sky. She'd worked as a waitress at the café with Amie. For a split second, I wondered if she'd planned to join in with the mocking hyenas' juvenile harassment. No, she didn't seem like the type. Maybe she had sought me out to let me know she blamed me for the death of her friend and coworker. I wouldn't fault her for that. But her face was sweet and her expression was one of concern rather than mockery or condemnation. "Angel, right?"

"Uh, yeah. Hi." It wasn't until I tried to straighten that I realized I had tears streaming down my face. Talk about humiliating. I was a round, soggy mess. "Sorry, I don't mean to be rude, I just...I have to get out of here."

"I saw what happened back there, chère. Let me help. Please. Come along with me, we'll get you inside and cleaned up. Then we'll have a nice lunch. My treat. You can just sit and rest your feet for a while, okay?"

Lunch? She said the magic word. Despite my stomach being in knots, I still felt ravenous. Although, I wasn't sure I was in the right frame of mind for company. As I met her eyes, though, I recognized my own grief reflected there. We shared the same sense of sorrow. Well, maybe not *exactly* the same, but we were both mourning Amie and Jeremiah. Sky had been near the front of the crowd at the funeral, standing close to Amie's parents. Suddenly, it felt like a relief to be around someone I could commiserate with. Someone who'd known Amie. Someone who also felt a loss. Someone with kind eyes.

I contemplated the situation while minutes passed. Finally, Sky gently broke the silence with further persuasion. "Okay? A bathroom and then lunch? A healthy lunch. My mate is at a table just inside that restaurant right across the street." She gently grasped my arm and gestured back the way I'd come, back toward the crepe truck. It was then that I noticed a small bistro, Amandine's. "He was ready to set those loudmouthed doodoo-for-brains morons who were messing with you straight, but I made him stay inside. A good thing, too. What he'd've done to them would not have been pretty."

I let her pull me toward the restaurant, but I stopped once I realized how fancy it was inside. "I...I can't go inside. I—"

"No worries, chère. You and I will head straight to the bathroom. It's okay. Nothing to be embarrassed about. You're pregnant, and I've had some experience with that lately. One of my best friends is pregnant right now, too. Big as a house. Between you and me, she's had little accidents a few times."

Feeling tired and defeated from the stress of the day, I gave in and let her pull me through the restaurant and inside the bathroom, a small cubby labeled *cabbin*—Cajun slang for bathroom. She locked the door, closing us in together, and grabbed something out of her purse.

"I always carry wet wipes. My nephews are too old to need them now, but old habits die hard." She handed me a purse-sized pack of baby wipes—the good kind with aloe and lanolin—then turned her back to me to give me a hint of privacy, as though I hadn't already maxed out of the mortification department. "Go ahead."

Quickly, I used the wipes to clean myself. My panties were toast. I tugged them off and tossed them in the trash before washing out my shoes and drying them as best I could with paper towels and the automatic hand dryer. Once I was relatively clean and feeling a little less like a social outcast, I met Sky's eyes in the mirror and forced a smile. "Thank you."

She nodded. "Of course. Come on, now. Let's get some chow. This place has amazing etouffee."

"I don't want to interrupt your lunch with your..." What had she called him? "Your, uh, did you say *mate?*"

She laughed and waved me off. "I call him that. As in soulmate. And you're not interrupting a thing. It's a rough day for all of us. We'll both be grateful for your company."

I had to admit, her kindness was addicting. For some reason, maybe it was our mutual connection to Amie, she seemed to want to be friends, and I was sorely lacking in the friend department. Sorely. *For good reason*, I reminded myself. I was hungry both for food and camaraderie, and the set of Sky's jaw made it clear she was not about to take no for an answer.

Sky pulled me along as she weaved through small round tables of diners and headed to a spot in the back corner. I followed with only a slight reservation. I didn't know her, but maybe we would get to know each other, and then maybe we would like each other, and then maybe, just maybe, we would become friends. The thought of having a friend was as terrifying to me as it was thrilling.

I was getting ahead of myself, reading too much into her act of kindness. *Take it slow, Angel. Have a nice lunch and hopefully you can talk about Amie and Jeremiah and find out more about them.* Or maybe that wasn't a good idea.

Sky's mate was a giant of a man. He stood when we approached and kissed her—not a *glad-you're-back-I-missed-you* kiss. No, it was an *I-haven't-seen-you-for-decades-and-I-want-to-ravenously-devour-you* kiss. As I watched, I blushed from my toes to my crown. It didn't appear as though he was going to stop, either, until I cleared my throat and faked a cough to remind them I was standing right there.

Sky laughed and pulled away. "Save it for later, big guy."

His eyes were intense as he turned them on me and sized me up.

I wiggled my fingers in a little wave while biting back a completely unhinged laugh. There was something about the man's raw masculinity, his animal dominance that, instead of frightening me, made me feel safer. He looked as though he would be vicious under the right circumstance. But in this circumstance, he was on my side. Which meant no one would mess with me on his watch. And if there was any doubt about that, he squashed it when he spoke.

"If you would like me to char those fools out there to a crisp and devour their ashes, I will gladly do so."

O-kaaay. I was temporarily rendered speechless and stood staring at him like a gaping idiot, but Sky's admiration for him was evident. She scooted into his side, her eyes warm as she looked up at him. "This is my mate, Beast."

Beast? Fitting name.

Sky motioned to the chair across from her and I sat, running a shaky hand through my short, curly hair. Presenting myself as a friendly, likable person might be more difficult a task than I was capable of right then. I wasn't sure I was either friendly or likable. I wanted to be, at least in front of Sky and Beast. I wanted to be the kind of woman who attracted friendships. It took a lot of effort sometimes to act like a fully functioning adult.

"I'm Angel. Nice to meet you both."

"Let's get some food in you. You're eating for two. What do you like? Any crazy cravings?"

I glanced at the menu and saw a sample platter of fried seafood. "Fried. I crave anything and everything fried."

Sky patted my hand and waved at a waitress passing by. "You got it. Anything fried sounds like dinner at our house every night. I have teenage nephews. I can't get Nick and Casey to even look at a vegetable unless I batter and deep fry it. Lately, their favorite meal is deep-fried hot pockets."

Sky cringed at the thought, but I sighed aloud imagining how deliciously crispy and greasy and heavenly a fried hot pocket would be. Why had I never thought of that?

She laughed reading my expression. "They'd love you."

The waitress stopped by and took our orders before hurrying away. She was right back with a sweet tea for me and a basket of big, warm, freshly baked rolls for the table.

I grabbed one and took a bite, not at all shy when it came to food. "I feel like I have a tapeworm inside of me. I just want to eat constantly."

Sky grinned. "Do you know what you're having?"

The bread was suddenly extra thick in my mouth. I took a drink of tea to help swallow it down. "A girl."

"Congratulations! Have you picked out a name yet?"

I shook my head and picked at the bread on my plate. "Um, no. I haven't. I just call her Baby Girl."

Quiet fell over the table, and when I looked up, Sky seemed to be contemplating something. "I don't mean to rude, and it's really none of my business, but I've seen you in the diner a few times and I noticed you at the funeral this morning... Is the... I mean, are you..."

Sky struggled with the question, but Beast did not. "Where is your young's father?"

"Oh." My cheeks were suddenly on fire. I hated to lie, but really, what choice did I have? Besides, Sky was right, it wasn't any of their business. "He's out of the picture. Permanently. You see, Amie and Jeremiah—"

"They sort of adopted you." Sky was nodding like she'd just fit the pieces of a puzzle together.

"Well, not exactly..." What could I say? Not the truth. I wasn't ready to divulge that. Besides, I didn't think I could handle shouldering the shame and guilt that I would certainly feel if the truth was revealed and these nice people's gazes turned from concerned and caring to angry and blaming.

"Of course. they did. It makes perfect sense. I mean, Amie and I didn't talk a whole lot about our personal lives outside of work, but I did know she and Jeremiah had infertility issues and were trying desperately to get pregnant. It makes perfect sense she'd want to be close to you and share this with you—be there for you so you don't have to go through the experience alone. Amie was a good friend like that." Sky's eyes filled with tears and her voice cracked. "I suppose it was a good thing it never happened for them. It would be awful if they'd left a child behind to grow up without them."

I sucked in a sharp breath and stood up abruptly. My belly knocked into the table, and I gasped as my tea splashed out over the rim of the glass and onto the white tablecloth. "I-I'm so sorry. I just remembered I have a thing I forgot about. It's urgent. An urgent thing, yeah. I have to go."

As fast as I could, I waddled across the bistro, through the front door, down the sidewalk, huffing and puffing. By the time I reached my car, which was parked back at the church parking lot, I was exhausted and covered in sweat. I climbed into the ten-year-old Lincoln Town Car I'd inherited from my late uncle, and headed out of New Orleans like the devil was nipping at my heels.

I should have known better than to think I could socialize and make friends. Terrible idea, especially with anyone who had also known Amie.

Chapter Three

ARMAND

The redheaded female slobbering in my ear was needy and begging to be fucked. She ran her tongue over the shell of my ear and purred like a cat. She was attractive enough—large breasts, lush curves—and she smelled okay. A bit too much like artificial strawberries for my taste. She was...nice.

I held her by the back of her head and kissed her deeply, sucking her tongue into my mouth, fighting, yearning, to feel a spark—something, anything.

Nothing.

I pulled away, nudging her to give me some elbow room. "Sorry, I am not interested."

She laughed and slapped my arm playfully. "Come on. We can go back to my place. My roommate is out of town, and we'll have the whole place to ourselves."

"No, thank you."

When she finally realized I was serious, she scowled at me and, muttering something under her breath, stormed off to the other end of the bar. Not a bad reaction. I had received everything from a slap across the face to having a drink poured over my head, or being threatened within an inch of my life. No matter. I was not to be sidetracked from the desperate, exhaustive search for my mate. Most of the other dragons had found their mates by simply stumbling upon them. Not me. I'd been searching for months, repeatedly frequenting every bar within a fifty-mile radius—from the shot-and-a-beer dives to the fancy piano lounges—and was having all the luck of a broken mirror.

I motioned for the bartender to bring me another beverage and turned to scan the room again on the off chance I had missed a potential mate. No. I had already kissed, spoken to, or flirted with every unmated female in the place, and with each, I'd felt every bit of nothing.

"What was wrong with that one?" Ovide plopped down heavily next to me and nodded at the bartender for a beer. "She looked just your type."

I cocked my head and narrowed my eyes at him. "My type?"

"Not picky."

"Your humor is world-class, Ovide. You should be one of those stand-up comedians." I took a swig of my beer. It tasted like watered-down urine. "I don't know why I continue to visit every alcoholic establishment within miles to sit at the bar and pay for this swill that doesn't have a chance of intoxicating me."

"Because you are desperate, my brother."

"Aren't you? We are closing in on the eclipse and neither of us has found a mate. Do you not care that our friends will have to put us down if we don't find mates? That otherwise, we'll ended up insane?"

Ovide paid for his beer and upended it, drinking it down in one go. "I do not care."

Cranky sonofabitch. "Why are you here, then?"

"Looking for you, of course. I need something that's going to ease the dullness of this world in a real way." He stood and nodded at me. "Besides, if that redhead is a virgin, I am the Queen of England. Are you finished for the evening?"

I glanced around the bar once more and shrugged. Might as well call it a night. The evening was another loss. "Yes. Again, there is no one here for me."

"When you find your mate, it just hits you, brother. You don't have to stick your tongue down her throat as a test to see if she's the one. You'll know."

He spoke as though he had more to say about the subject—something he was choosing to keep hidden. "What do you know about it?"

With a bitter laugh, he stepped out onto the street and looked around. "More than I care to."

I followed him into the shadows behind the bar and after carefully casing the area, we each transformed and took flight.

When we flew, there was always the possibility that we might be spotted by humans, but we'd learned long ago that the threat was minimal. Of those who saw us, most convinced themselves that we couldn't be real, that their minds were playing tricks on them. They assured themselves that what they saw was an optical illusion—a small plane or a large bird. There were those rare few who were not deceived by their own rationality, but they either knew better than to say anything or were dismissed as being delusional when they did speak up.

We flew high above the little town, heading toward my castle located on a small island just off the coast. My castle was secluded, and I was happy I'd found the location and claimed it before any of the other dragons. It was bigger than I needed because, out of boredom, I'd continuously remodeled and added rooms to it over the years. I had way too much free time and not enough tasks to fill it.

With some of my free time, I'd taken to brewing spirits. There was a little stone building at the back of the island that I used as a brewery. It was in the small brick building that I'd built the system I used to make my special intoxicating beverages. It was a hobby I'd learned in the old world and further refined in this new world. The others appreciated my tinkering and experimenting with flavors and ingredients, as nothing in this new world had any inebriating effect on a dragon. Lately, it had become something to keep my mind off the chore of visiting bars hoping to find my mate.

I landed before Ovide and grabbed a pair of spare jeans I kept hooked on a nail just inside the brew building. When he landed, we entered the single-roomed space, and I pointed out the nearest shelves stocked with my latest creation. It tasted like pears, and only a small amount was needed to fulfill its objective, as our fellow dragon, Remy, had learned from experience. It had worked its magic on him, enough that he'd flown straight into a brick wall. Which was a good thing because that was how he'd found his mate. Lucky firemouth.

The room was full of shelving units housing jars of ingredients and flasks of brew from older batches—flasked, corked, and shelved for rainy days and thirsty dragons. Ovide was thirstier than the rest of us, it seemed.

"Pick your poison."

He scanned the shelves, then grabbed a couple of bottles of the new stuff. "This will do."

"What is it with you, brother?"

"What do you mean? All's well." He moved to leave and then stopped. "No. All is not well. We have spent nearly a hundred years together, the six of us, in this cesspool of a world. A hundred years. And, in less than a year, nearly all of us are mated."

"You and I will find our mates as well, Ovide."

He shook his head and shot me a dark look. "You? Yes. You will find someone. Me? Never. My chance has come and gone."

I followed him out and rubbed at my chin. "What are you talking about, brother?"

He didn't look back at me. "Thank you for the brew. I will see you in a few days."

He shifted into his dragon form, then scooped the bottles and held them gently in his mouth. I watched silently as he took to the sky, growing smaller and smaller with distance. Something was off about Ovide, I thought as I headed toward my house. He'd always been either gloomy and pensive or downright ill-tempered and disagreeable, but more so lately than ever before. I'd always assumed his moping irritability was simply his nature, but it was getting worse.

None of us dragons had known each other well in the old world. We were each from different kingdoms and different lands. We only met after we fled our home world to search out a new place to live.

I let myself into the backdoor of my castle. The entire back wall of the place was floor-to-ceiling glass. It afforded me a spectacular view, and I stared out across the expanse of the ocean. It was a calm night with a large almost-full moon reflecting off the gentle waves. Every few years, a hurricane blew out the glass, and I had to replace it all over again. Not that I minded. It was something to do.

I stared at the night sky, searching for any last trace of Ovide. He seemed to grow darker and darker with each of our dragon brothers' mating. I understood, in a way, I supposed. It was difficult to be one of only two dragons still waiting, wandering and wondering, searching for a mate and hoping one even existed. Seeing the rest of my brothers with their mates was like a steel dagger through the heart. I'd never admit that I wanted a mate, but of course, I did. As the days grew closer to the eclipse, I felt more and more as though half of me was missing.

Sighing deeply, I stripped my jeans off and strode toward the walk-in shower in the master bathroom. I needed to wash off the sickly scent of artificial strawberries.

Chapter Four

ANGEL

Before Amie's death, I'd made it a habit to stop by to the Bon Temps Café where she and Sky worked at least once or twice a week. I liked sitting at the counter and watching Amie. It gave me chance to evaluate the type of person she was. A good one. I'd watched her mop up spilled cokes from careless customers and wield complaints from nitpicky ones. I'd watched her treat her regulars like family and welcome new customers with a warm smile and a kind word.

Although, none of that mattered anymore. Now that her life had been so tragically cut short. The café had lost a great waitress, the world had lost a stellar human being, and I had lost a friend.

It was Thursday and I found myself, as per my usual routine, entering the café at around the tail end of the lunch rush. I wiggled onto my normal seat at the counter with just barely enough clearance for my belly. It had been three days since the funeral and my thoughts and emotions were still in turmoil. It had not been an easy week. To top it off, the video of people taunting me as I wet myself had gone viral. Well, not viral, but viral as far as our locality. I was the infamous Angel of Death in our tiny bayou town as it was. The urination incident had only added fuel to the fire.

Besides dealing with the fallout from the video, I was just...confused.

The bottom had fallen out of my world. Baby Girl was growing bigger each day, and I was scared. What would become of her? All the plans I'd made for her—plans that had been set in motion to ensure her a bright future surrounded by a loving, caring family—were gone. It was left up to me to figure out which path to take next to ensure her a secure future. I was in charge of building a life for another human being. Me. Wasn't that a joke?

I ran my fingers along the counter in front of me and tried to think. I couldn't seem to sift through all the sludge in my brain. I was exhausted and hormonal and depressed and all I wanted to do was stay hidden at home—shut away from the gossip slingers. It was Thursday, though—café day. The only thing different was that this time, I came to see Sky, not Amie. I'd felt guilty for days about the way I'd run out on her and her, uh, *mate*, at Amandine's.

"Angel!" Sky appeared in front of me, a big smile not quite concealing the concern etched into her features. "I'm so glad to see you. I've been worried about you. Are you okay?"

I folded my hands on my lap and nodded. "Everything's fine." That, I'd learned long ago, was the acceptable response regardless of the truth.

"I was hoping you'd be in today. Let's see, if I remember correctly, Amie always served you a glass of milk, right?"

I nodded, surprised she'd noticed something like that. I supposed waitresses just notice what the regulars ordered even if you weren't the one serving them. "Actually, though, I came to see you. I wanted to apologize for running out the other day after the funeral—"

"No apology necessary. None at all. It was a stressful day for all of us and maybe more so for you in your condition."

"But still, I—"

"Not another word about it. I'm serious! Now, can I get you something to go with that milk?"

Sky was really nice. I had a feeling she was probably an awesome friend. "Sugar. Any kind." I looked down at the dessert stand.

She was back almost instantly with a glass of milk and a large slice of apple pie topped with a healthy scoop of vanilla ice cream. The ice cream was beginning to melt and leaking down the caramelized apples and soaking the pastry. "Here y'are. As requested, sugar. This is the best pie today. Freshly baked and still warm. Just came out of the oven."

I pulled the plate closer and shoveled a large bite of warm apples and cold ice cream into my mouth. Heavenly. I took another bite and then another, and the next thing I knew, the pie was gone. I pressed the tines of my fork down, squashing the crumbs onto them to get every last morsel.

"There's more where that came from. Would you care for another slice?"

I shook my head, slightly embarrassed. I was already as big as a heifer and with swollen ankles, feet, wrists, and hands. "I'm not one of those women who work out throughout their pregnancy."

Sky raised an eyebrow. "Those women are real? I thought that kind of thing was only staged for those housewives shows."

I smiled, probably the first in a week. "I wouldn't know. Maybe they are just fictional."

"Tell you what, if you want to start a petition protesting false representation of pregnant women in the movies and television, I'll commit to going door to door for signatures—seein' as how you can't walk too well and all."

A surprisingly hearty belly laugh escaped past my lips, and I covered my mouth when a few heads turned my way. My cheeks heated, and my gaze met Sky's smiling eyes. "I didn't mean to laugh like that. It's just...god, it seems like it's been forever since I laughed. I don't get out much."

Sky watched me with a curious expression as she cut another slice of the pie and placed it between us. "How about we make a deal? I pay for both slices of this pie and, in exchange, you come to my place for dinner tomorrow night? We're having a barbecue."

I paused. The pie was mighty good, and one slice hadn't made a dent in my sweet tooth. But I didn't do dinner at people's houses. In all fairness, I didn't usually have people to do dinner with. I started to shake my head, but Sky pulled the pie away from me.

"Dinner or no pie. That's the deal. C'mon, it'll be fun. A couple of other pregnant friends will be there. They're twins and both pregnant at the same time; isn't that funny?"

A dinner with other pregnant women gushing about how happy they are and making plans for the future? No, thanks. "I'm sorry. I'm just..."

"Bad at making excuses to get out of dinner?" She laughed, then her voice got serious. "Look, chère, I know you and Amie were close, and you look like you have the weight of the world on your shoulders. I'd like to help, is all. I'd love for you and me to become friends. So, whaddaya say? Come over? I'll send Beast to pick you up."

"Really, Sky, it's nice of you to think about me, but—"

"Wonderful!" She threw her hands in the air in exclamation. "So, just write your address down for me, and he'll be there at six tomorrow night. Our place is only accessible by boat. It's in the middle of the swamp. But don't let that dissuade you. It's not a dilapidated shack, I promise. It'll be fun, and I'll make sure to have something fried and lots of sugary desserts."

I slumped and grabbed the pie from her. "Fine."

"Address."

Frowning, I scribbled it down on a napkin and slid it across to her. "Thank you for inviting me," I monotoned.

She laughed, completely unoffended by my lack of enthusiasm.

I was dreading it already. The only enjoyable evening to me was one spent with my pajamas in bed. "I can get myself there, though. I have a boat. Just give me your address."

She laughed. "No, ma'am. Beast will pick you up and drop you off later. You look like a runner, and I'm not letting you bail on me. Trust me, you can't run from Beast. The man is a bloodhound in a man's body." She waved the slip of napkin with my address at me and grinned. "My bloodhound will pick you up tomorrow, around six."

I looked down at my pie and frowned. She hadn't given me ice cream with this slice."

Reading my expression, she pulled it away from me with a knowing look. "Forgot the ice cream, huh? Yes, I can take a hint."

I had to doubt that.

Chapter Five

ANGEL

Beast arrived at six sharp. He stared at my home with a bewildered look, and I could tell he was curious. But to his credit, he didn't ask.

My home, Magnolia Plantation, was a grand place meant to hold a large family and a full staff of servants. Too bad there was only me. I had inherited the antebellum mansion, which was ridiculously huge and drafty for someone who lived alone. Most of it was just a place to collect cobwebs and harbor ghosts—room after room of expensive antiques. I'd considered selling the place, but where would I go? Nowhere that had any neighbors in close proximity, that was for sure. I preferred seclusion and my home provided it, so I stayed.

Beast met me halfway to the mud boat and then helped me as I clumsily climbed in. He caught me by the elbows and eased me down onto the bench seat.

Beast's brows furrowed and he rubbed the back of his neck. "I do not think a boat is the most comfortable form of transportation for a female such as you."

"Such as me?"

He gestured to my stomach pointedly.

I had to laugh. Shrugging, I shifted to get comfortable on the hard plank seat. "I told Sky I'd find my own way, but she insisted. I guess she didn't trust me to show up."

"Would you have shown up?"

"Hell, no. I had my pajamas already laid out on the bed."

He let out a roar of laughter and nodded. "Okay, then."

We rode the rest of the way in silence, down small waterways and through creeks that were almost just mud puddles. Then we were all of a sudden deep in the swamp and the sun was shining through the trees just right and I did not regret being in that boat. Not at all. It was a little hard on the butt cheeks, but other than that, I loved being so deep in the bayou.

As Beast navigated the tall grass and cattails like a pro, I sighed and tipped my face up to study the canopy of cypress branches overhead. They were strewn with low-hanging Spanish moss. The whole scene reminded me of pictures of prehistoric eras—like a land frozen in time. I imagined time ceasing to exist in a place like this.

The silence between us was comfortable as we made our way through the swamp. Just after we made the turn through an arch formed by the root system of a very old, very dead tree, the water opened up to a large lake and an even larger house, I glanced back at Beast and nodded. "Wow. I had no idea you lived in a castle."

He snorted. "You live in a castle as well."

"I live in a plantation home, not a castle."

"Potato, tomato."

I tilted my head and studied him. "Huh?"

"Potato, tomato. Either way I say it, it is the same thing."

I bit back a laugh. "A potato is not the same thing as a tomato. No matter how you say it."

He frowned. "I am not the best at these modern sayings."

"Modern sayings? How old are you?"

His gaze strayed to something over my shoulder. The huge smile that stretched across his face told me Sky was behind me. He sure did light up for the woman who called him her soulmate. "Angel has asked old I am."

"Older than dirt." Sky smiled at me when I turned to her. "I'm so glad you made it!" she said as though I'd had a choice.

Climbing out of the boat proved to be a challenge since my huge stomach limited how high I could lift my legs. In the end, Beast scooped me under the arms like I was a toddler and lifted me onto the deck. When I was standing on solid ground, I glowered at them both. "That was mortifying. If you'd have let me boat myself over, I wouldn't have had an audience for that."

Sky grinned. "If I'd have let you boat yourself over, you'd have stayed home."

Beast wrapped his arms around Sky. "I missed you." Then he proceeded to make out with her right there in front of me. After a few minutes, it became uncomfortable, and I cleared my throat loudly.

"Oh, sorry! We get carried away into our own little world sometimes. My nephews tease us all the time." Sky took my hand and pulled me toward the house. "Come on. I can't wait for you to meet everyone."

"Everyone?"

"Yeah. Almost. Ovide won't show, but he's a party pooper anyway. And Armand swore he'd come, but he's not here yet, so I'm not counting on him either." She squeezed my hand. "You look absolutely glowing, by the way."

I stared at the side of her head like she was crazy. I looked like a whale who was one plankton appetizer from a Jenny Craig before pic. Whaley Craig, maybe; glowing, not so much.

"You can look at me like that all you want. It's true. You're radiant."

I just ignored her. She was probably one of *those* women, the ones who felt like they had to say something nice and encouraging to the fat, pregnant goth-looking chick who appeared depressed all the time. I knew better, though. I owned mirrors.

Before I was mentally prepared for it, Sky was ushering me into a house full of people.

A beautiful, dark-skinned and very pregnant woman came rushing toward me. "You must be Angel! I'm Cherry!" She *was* glowing. And, if the smile on her face was any indication, she was one happy, fulfilled woman. She almost attempted to hug me before laughing it off and extending her hand instead. "Yeah, I don't think a welcome hug is going to work here. Not with these baby-incubators." She gestured from my belly to hers.

Another woman who looked nearly identical to Cherry with the exception of having a slightly smaller baby mound came over. She pointed to her stomach. "I don't know about you, but sometimes this thing is like a genie lamp beckoning everyone to 'rub here' like they can make a wish. I'm so over being touched and patted and rubbed."

"You love it when I touch and pat and rub you, Chyna." A giant of a man with flaming red hair wrapped his arm around her and leaned down and nuzzled her neck.

She wiggled as his nose tickled her. "I love it from you." She grinned up at the guy. "I don't love it from strangers."

As I stood there watching the lovefest, a large, blonde man came over to Cherry. Were all these men giants? He tenderly wrapped an arm around her and persuaded her to get off her feet by leading her to the nearest chair and helping her lower herself into it.

Oh, gag. Had I stepped onto a Hallmark movie set?

Feeling out of my element and a little like a fifth wheel, I fake-coughed to get their attention. "When a stranger tries to touch my stomach, I pretend to have a contraction." I let out a wail like I was in the midst of a labor pain and doubled over as much as my bulbous middle would allow.

"No way!" Cherry's hand flew over her mouth to cover her giggles.

"Ha! I love it! I'll have to try that." Chyna contorted her face like she was in agony and bent over grunting.

"What the—" Another woman came into the room from what appeared to be the kitchen clutching her chest. "Chyna, are you alright?"

Chyna straightened. "Fine. Angel was just showing us how to play keep away with touchy-feely strangers."

The woman's gaze shifted to me. "I'm Lennox, Remy's mate...I mean, uh, fiancée." She held out her hand and as we walked toward one another, I reached to take the hand she offered, only I didn't quite make it.

My foot hit the throw rug just right—or wrong as it were—and while I didn't exactly hit the ground, I did go halfway down with one leg spayed one way and the other leg turned out in the opposite direction. My graceful pose wasn't even the most humiliating thing. Nope. The worst part was the ear-splitting screechy scream I let out. It sounded like the cry of a wounded piglet that had swallowed a puppy's squeaky toy.

There were gasps. People came running. But, holding up my hands, I waved everyone off and wiggled like an octopus amputee as I tried to get my legs back under me—the right way. I felt my back protest. "Oh, fuck."

I laughed to keep from crying as the pain coursed down my spine. I reached out to grab whatever was closest to me—which happened to be Sky's skirt. Sky had to quickly catch her waistband to keep it from coming down. I'd apologize later.

"Ok, I give up, help me up."

Bless Lennox and Sky. They were suddenly on either side of me, easing me up. By the time I was vertical again, I was praying a hole would open up and swallow me.

"That was mortifying."

Sky opened her mouth to say something, but before she could, there was a loud crash that made us all jump. I felt the energy in the room shift all of a sudden. I cringed, afraid to turn around. Every hair on my body stood on end. I froze and kept my eyes on Cherry's shoulder, ignoring the fact that the room had gone silent.

I had no clue what was going on in Beast's castle when I landed, but the scream from within pierced my very soul. A cry for help had alerted the most primal part of my being and sent my dragon into a fury. I took out Beast's door without a second of hesitation. My concern—my only concern—was coming to the aid of the female in need. That meant shifting back from my dragon form and entering Beast's abode by whatever means necessary.

And there, inside, was the most exquisite sight my eyes had ever beheld. A female, flanked on either side by Lennox and Sky who each held one of her arms keeping her steady.

I wanted to rush over and demand to know what had happened, who had hurt her, but all I could do was gape in awe at the stunning human female.

"You broke our door." Beast didn't sound overly upset, merely as though he was stating a fact.

Sky grinned at me. "S'up Armand? Did Angel's little slip scare you, too?"

As the woman called Angel slowly turned, I was struck with a maelstrom of emotions. My cock instantly hardened, and my hands ached to touch her. My dragon clawed at my skin wanting out. He longed to go to her, to care for her, guard her, protect her, and most of all, kill whoever had hurt her. Instinct came over me like a tidal wave, and I took an unbalanced step toward her.

"Release her." Was all I could say.

Sky and Lennox gaped at me, glanced at one another, looked back at me, and both released their grips simultaneously and raised their hands in a gesture of innocence.

Angel. She looked like an angel. Coal-black hair, black-painted fingernails and toenails, dark eye makeup. It wasn't until her hands moved to rest on her stomach that I noticed that she was very pregnant, and a fierce possessiveness rippled through me.

Protect her. My dragon insisted. But...that was crazy. She clearly wasn't mine to protect.

I stood gaping and when our eyes met, I felt a tingle of electricity shoot straight to my toes.

"Why are you...umm..." She began to address me, then her cheeks turned bright red and she looked at Sky. "He's...*naked?*"

It was only then that I realized I'd been so worried about conquering the foe and rescuing the beautiful Angel that I hadn't paid a thought to the fact that I was unclothed in the presence of humans. I quickly used both hands to shield my cock as I looked at Lennox and Sky apologetically.

Chyna let out a little giggle. "Angel, meet Armand. Armand, meet Angel."

Sky was giving me the stink eye, which I ignored. Beast disappeared, probably to get me some clothes.

The amazing beauty wet her lips and folded her arms under her breasts. That pushed them up higher, and they looked like they were seconds from spilling out of the blouse she wore. "Hi. I'd shake your hand, but..."

I tore my eyes from her cleavage, suddenly realizing how ridiculous I must look to her. Breaking down a door, attending a gathering naked. Feeling quite foolish, I accepted the clothes Beast silently offered and nodded. "Hello. I am usually clothed."

Beast snorted, and I scowled at him. Bastard.

"I... Excuse me for one moment." I directed my words to Angel, not caring what Sky, Lennox, Cherry, or anyone else thought of my manners. Then I turned and quickly donned the jeans and T-shirt from Beast.

"I think your scream startled Armand. I've never seen him look so...out of sorts." Cherry spoke to Angel then raised her eyebrows at me. "Have you been sampling your own goods, Armand?"

I spun. "I have not been imbibing. I am simply concerned." I focused on the blushing, round female. "Please tell me what it is that elicited such a scream from your beautiful lips? Has something hurt you? Or frightened you? I will destroy it."

"Uh, I tripped over the rug." She raised her hand. "Clumsy pregnant woman here."

That would not do. Rugs that could be tripped over were much too dangerous to have around a female in her condition. I snatched up the offending rug, then gathered the one in the hall and the one near the front door and, as the rest of the group watched, marched them outside and tossed them into the swamp. When I returned, they were all staring at me with open mouths.

"Alrighty." Lenni rested her hand on Angel's shoulder and made a face. "Well, this is weird."

Sky's hands flew to her hips. "Dammit, Armand. Now you owe us a front door and three throw rugs!" She let out an exasperated breath. "Let's just get ready to eat. I made a dozen sides and Beast tried to grill."

"Tried to? Female, I grilled."

"He tries, but he just flash-flames everything." Sky laughed and moved into the open kitchen.

I lost track of everyone as Angel's eyes met mine. She looked away quickly, but then her gaze was drawn right back to me. Her cheeks remained a beautiful shade of pink, but those hazel eyes stayed firm. Her chin rose in a look of subtle defiance that provoked my dragon even more. He tore at my skin, wanting desperately to be closer to her.

I gave in and took a few steps closer until Angel had to tilt her head back to hold my gaze. That chin still rose challengingly and it sent a thrill through me like nothing I'd ever experienced

"You're staring. "There was just the smallest gap between her front two teeth that I noticed when she spoke.

"I cannot help myself. You are beautiful."

Her eyes widened and she took a step back.

A little creepy, *Armand*, Cherry communicated telepathically to me, as well as every dragon present.

Angel turned to leave and brushed against me. The slight gasp that escaped her lips told me that she was feeling the same pull I was. Energy coursed from the spot she'd touched.

I reached out and cupped her elbow, keeping her where she was, prolonging the sensation. I didn't know what to say. I'd never felt anything like the fierce possessiveness that took hold of me. With a desperation I could not explain, I wanted to care for her and look after her. We stood frozen for a few awkward seconds. And then she said the words that turned the fire in my blood to ice.

"I have a boyfriend."

She blurted the words from her mouth as though she was throwing them at me. I was unable to control the low growl that emerged from my chest.

"Come over here, Angel! I want to show you something." Sky's voice broke through my haze.

Angel looked up into my eyes and pulled her arm back. She wet her lips again and then moved away. But, even when she was in the kitchen with Sky, she glanced over at me, her eyes as drawn to me as I was drawn to her.

I felt paralyzed by her. I couldn't help but stare. From her black-as-night hair to her black-painted toenails, she was more interesting than any female I'd ever laid eyes on. I took a step toward her and heard another one of her little intakes of breath.

I paused and stood rooted to the spot, unable to take my eyes from Angel. What male would be so careless with his pregnant female as to allow her to attend a gathering without him? It was a male's duty to look after and protect his female—especially one who was carrying his youngling in her belly. Yet, this beautiful, fragile human female was alone without her male present. That did not seem right. Not at all. Stupid male.

The duty of caring for a mate was an honor, a privilege not to be taken lightly. Any male who did not gladly and wholeheartedly accept that duty did not deserve his female. Angel's male clearly did not deserve her. She was out on her own, vulnerable to predators or other dangers of the world. Did he not know what an incredible gift a female such as this one was?

"You okay, brother?" Beast slapped me on the back and grunted. "You look as though you just saw a ghost."

"What?" I shook my head to try and clear it. "I have not seen a ghost in fifty years. What are you talking about?"

"It is a human expression."

No, I was not okay. I was drawn inexplicably to the pregnant human female, I was livid at her mate who was clearly shirking his duty and did not deserve her, and I was compelled to protect her as though she was mine. "I need something to drink."

He passed me a cup and winced when I threw it back straight. "That's the strong stuff."

I did not care. I needed it. What I was feeling made no sense. I wanted nothing more than to protect a female who couldn't possibly be my mate. I was going to need more than one strong drink. I was going to need a barrel.

Chapter Seven
ANGEL

Pregnancy hormones were nasty devils. Not the cute, chubby kind with little red horns and forked tails. I'm talking about the demented, demonic, satanic kind. I had come to fully expect the ups and downs—irrational anger one second, tears the next. And the increased sex drive...holy cow!

The interaction with Beast's friend, Armand, had caught me so off guard that my hands were still trembling. I couldn't help but lie about the boyfriend thing. It was the intense way he looked at me. As though he might devour me. Well, that and the fact that I was insanely attracted to him. Insanely. Of course, part of that was maybe because I'd seen every last bit of him and a big part of him had been, *ahem*, prominent. A very big part.

Who did that, though? Showed up naked to a barbecue? And why wasn't anyone else freaked out about it? Maybe he was a nudist. Maybe he was from California.

Anyhow, he had the most incredible tattoo of a dragon extending from one shoulder and down over the left side of his chest and ripped abs with the tail pointing right down to his "big part". The urge to throw myself on top of him and ride him like a cowgirl must have been a new side effect of the pregnancy hormones. I better watch that or I might find myself doing something I regretted. Not that it mattered, I mean I was about as attractive as a hippopotamus waddling around with my giant watermelon-belly and swollen ankles. Any man that desired me was seriously demented or had a bizarre fetish.

I blew out a slow breath and tried to focus on what Sky was rambling about. It had something to do with schools in the area and I felt like a jerk for not paying attention.

The guy was a perfect specimen of maleness, that was for sure—around six and a half feet tall, muscles on top of muscles, exuding an air of raw masculinity. Come to think of it, all three of the guys present had the same general physique. That was odd. Maybe they were all male models from the same agency. No, they seemed too masculine for that. Maybe bodybuilders or personal trainers? Although, Sky and Beasts home was enormous and beautifully decorated. I couldn't imagine a waitress and a personal trainer affording such a secluded mansion deep in the bayou. Mercenaries! That was it! They were soldiers of fortune—hired guns. I stifled a gasp when I realized the truth.

I glanced back at Armand and felt my blood pressure skyrocket. He was handsome, mysterious and dangerous—a trifecta. He looked masculine in a rugged, strong, tough way. As I studied the set of his square jaw, I noticed his eyes were riveted to me. *Gulp.* Did he just totally catch me checking him out? Or was he checking me out first and I caught him? As our eyes locked, there was something dominating, possessive, in his stare that my body deeply responded to. My knees went weak and my panties dampened. It was then that I realized that Armand was emitting a low growl.

Wait...*growl?*

"Angel?"

I snapped my head around to Sky and blinked a few times. What had she been saying? "I'm sorry, Sky. It's this pregnancy brain."

She raised her eyebrows, glanced over at Armand, then nodded knowingly. "I see."

I forced a smile and, pressing my shoulders back, rolled my neck to loosen the stiff muscles. "What were you saying?"

Sky wrinkled her brow in concern. "Is your back okay? You didn't hurt yourself when you slipped on the rug did you?"

"I'm fine. Just a little twinge is all."

"Do you need something for it? I don't know what you can take, but I have Tylenol and a few other things in the bathroom."

I waved her concern away. "I'm really fine. I promise."

"If you're sure..."

"I am." I turned my back to Armand so I could focus on Sky. "Thank you for inviting me today. I don't do stuff like this often." It was the closest I would come to admitting aloud that I never did anything with anyone because I was a loser who had no friends. No, worse than a loser. I was Angel of Death.

"I'm so glad you did. We should hang out more often."

"I'd like that." I felt genuinely thrilled by her suggestion.

"You know where to find me during the day, Angel." She gently touched my wrist and gave me a gentle smile. "I know you and Amie were friends, and I can only imagine she's looking down from heaven and approving of us getting together."

And that's when the bottom dropped out of my newfound friendship. In a heartbeat, I went from being thrilled to have Sky in my corner to feeling like a piece of crap. If Sky knew the truth, she'd probably send me on my way with explicit instructions never to contact her or set foot in the Bon Temps Café ever again.

I felt wretched. Like a wretched human being.

Sky must have noticed my change in mood because her brow wrinkled. "I'm sorry I soured your mood by bringing up Amie while we were having a good time. I guess it's too soon to reminisce casually without feeling awful, huh?"

I just shrugged, unable to get a response out over the thick lump in my throat.

"Well, are you hungry? You must be hungry eating for two. Cherry's always hungry. She eats everything in sight."

"I heard that!" Cherry's voice adopted a mock-stern tone. "It's one hundred percent true!" Her giggles carried from the other room.

I breathed a shaky laugh trying to keep my emotions on an even keel. "I'm always hungry, too."

Beast came up behind Sky and wrapped his hands around her waist. "You have made quite an impression, Angel." Beast gestured with his eyes to Armand who was still standing nearby. Still watching me intently through narrowed eyes. Still emitting the strange, low growl. A little scary.

Sky slipped away from her man and grabbed a couple of plates before calling everyone to head outside and eat. That was when Armand immediately stepped forward and grabbed two plates from the stack. "I will accompany you so you do not trip again."

"That's not necessary. I'll be more careful this time. Besides, you killed the rugs, remember?"

"I am not sorry."

"Also you're kinda like...growling. Are you pissed?" I wondered if it was because I'd told him I had a boyfriend. Truth be told, I felt a little guilty for lying. I'd just been so flustered it was the quickest way I could think of to turn down the heat between us. "Is it because I said I had a boyfriend?"

"Yes. I am pissed because he is not here with you, caring for you. He should be by your side. Anything could happen to you in your condition."

"I think I'm pretty safe now that the rugs are at the bottom of the swamp."

He just grunted.

"Okay, truth time. I don't really have a boyfriend. I don't know why I said that. I'm actually alone."

He studied me for a moment, his expression unreadable, before offering me his elbow. "Please, I have your plate, just take my arm."

When I hesitated, his look turned to pleading. He was hard to resist and I slipped my arm under his massive bicep.

Whoa. As soon as we made contact, heat flowed through my veins like lava. Little butterflies fluttered around inside me. I would have blamed the pregnancy hormones for the crazy reaction, but judging by the weird growly sounds coming from the big guy escorting me, he was as affected by our physical contact as I was.

Chapter Eight

ANGEL

The situation with Armand was bizarre to say the least—both his attention to me and my body's reaction to him. One, I wasn't a fragile figurine made of glass, and two, what the hell was wrong with my damned libido? Pregnancy hormones. Armand led me outside to a patio chair and motioned for me to sit in it.

"This is the most comfortable chair out here. You should have it."

"Yep," Sky called from where she was arranging the platters of meat and bowls of potato salad, hush puppies, beans and rice, slaw, and all kinds of yummy dishes. "He's right about the chair. It is an ergonomic exterior patio lounger and recliner."

My mouth watered at the spread Sky was laying out and I suddenly felt famished. "Thanks, Armand, looks like an awesome chair but I'd really like to get some food first."

"I will serve you food. Sit."

"You don't even know what I like!"

"I will bring you some of everything." He looked at my belly. "Three helpings of everything."

I barked a laugh. "Look, I appreciate how concerned you seem to be about the big clumsy pregnant woman, but I assure you, I'm perfectly capable of serving myself."

He stared at me as though he was thinking up a good comeback to use to argue with me, but before he could say anything, I snatched a plate from his hand and waddled over to the food table.

Armand followed closely behind.

As I began filling my plate, I understood Sky's comment about Beast's grilling. The meat was completely blackened on the outside and raw on the inside. That didn't stop me from piling my plate high. I was in line behind Cherry, with Armand hovering over my shoulder. He'd abandoned his still empty plate on the end of the table and followed me. He was holding his hands poised on either side of me, only inches from my elbows as though ready to catch me if I so much as stumbled. He probably though he'd better guard the bumbling oaf before she falls and files a lawsuit. Or worse, hurts the baby somehow. My blood ran cold at the thought. My worst fear—that my curse would affect Baby Girl and something terrible would happen to her. Oh, god, I shuddered at the thought.

The most important task I'd ever had—the one I had devoted every fiber of my being to completing successfully, was caring for the little growing fetus inside until she was a life independent of me. I would do everything to keep her healthy and, most of all, *alive*. No small task for Angel of Death.

"Are you sure that is enough? Perhaps you should try to eat more. Shall I fill you a second plate?" Armand's questions cut through my morbid, fear-based thoughts.

A second plate? My eyes bugged out, and I eyed Armand like he'd just grown another limb. Then I looked down at my plate piled high with a mountain of potato salad, a fat, juicy steak, hush puppies, a cupcake a couple cookies, and a little of every other delicious fatty, sweet, or fried food available. Was he kidding? Was he making fun of my pregnant appetite? But his expression carried no hint of sarcasm or humor. In fact, he looked sincerely concerned.

"I'm pretty sure I've got more than I can fit in my stomach in one sitting. In fact, I think I may have overdone it a little." I glanced around self-consciously. When I glimpsed Cherry's plate, though, hers was heaped just as high as mine which made me feel slightly better about my own gluttonous appetite.

Armand followed me like white on rice to the comfy ergo-whatever chair. He one-armed a stone table, hefting it into the air and placing it in front of me like it weighed nothing. Those bulging muscles weren't just for show.

It wasn't until I sat down that I realized I'd forgotten to get something to drink.

"Darn." I debated whether or not I wanted to get up again. Maybe I'd just skip the beverage.

"What is the matter?" Armand's concern was evident as he studied me.

"No biggie. I forgot to get a drink is all."

"I will get your drink. What would you like? Lemonade, soda, water, iced tea, Kool-Aid, milk, orange juice?"

I laughed. "I didn't see all of that up there. Orange juice? Was there orange juice? Did I miss it?"

"If you want orange juice, only say the word, I will travel to the grocery store and buy you orange juice."

Chyna snickered. "I'm surprised he didn't offer to squeeze the oranges himself."

Armand frowned at her then turned back to me. "I will squeeze oranges and make you fresh orange juice."

That got a chuckle out of everyone but me. Armand glared at the others, and I felt my cheeks heat. His over-attentiveness was beginning to get embarrassing.

I jutted out my chin defiantly. "For your information, women have been pregnant and giving birth since the beginning of time. We're not so fragile that we need to be coddled and waited on."

Armand looked as though I'd stolen his puppy. "Are you saying you do not want my help?"

I eyed the drinks table.

The ergo-something chair was super comfortable.

The drinks table wasn't far, but "far" was a relative term.

"I'll have lemonade."

Chapter Nine

ANGEL

Armand was back in no time settling into a chair next to mine with my lemonade, and his own plate piled high with food. He seemed to sit closer to me than felt normal. I sensed his heat radiating out and stroking my skin until I felt like fanning myself. The scent of him, like fresh rain and cedarwood, tickled my nostrils.

When Armand moved next to me, his thigh brushed against mine. I gritted my teeth as a shot of arousal tore through me. The others were chattering away—about what, I had no idea. I was too busy focusing on ignoring Armand and the effect his close proximity had on my nutty sex drive to notice.

He still seemed angry. I kept my eyes on my plate and my thighs pressed firmly together. Halfway through my plate, I was unable to ignore him anymore. I glanced up and met his eyes. They were a shocking royal purple. I'd never seen anyone with bright purple eyes before.

My fists automatically tightened and my fork banged against my plate drawing attention. Passing an apologetic smile across to Chyna and her boyfriend, Blaise, I turned slightly to Armand. "You still look angry. Why?"

Armand stretched his arm along the back of my chair and leaned close. "You deserve to be cared for. The male who impregnated and left you alone should be made to pay for such a terrible thing. I would like to find him and tear his heart out through his throat. I will do just that if you allow me to avenge you."

Crazy, but my first reaction was to be flattered. Then the truth in Armand's words smacked me upside the head. My hands began to tremble and I dropped them onto my lap to hide them. I took a big breath of air and blew it out slowly.

The urge to cry burned the back of my eyes, but I forced it down and swallowed around the lump in my throat. The last thing I wanted was to cry in front of all these people I'd just met. But it didn't seem as though I was going to be able to stop it. I rolled myself off the chair and took off at a fast waddle. I just hoped I could make it to the bath-room before the floodgates were loosed. Damned pregnancy hormones.

———

Armand

I was angry as hell. What kind of idiotic fool would abandon a beau-tiful female such as her? Especially one ripe with his child. The thought angered me so intensely I wanted find the moron and shred his flesh from his bones.

Angel had gone cold next to me, though. When I looked at her, she wouldn't look back at me. When I brushed against her thigh, she didn't react. She ate in silence and kept her eyes away from mine.

It was strange how her mood swing had altered mine. I felt upset and irritable. I wanted her attention back. I wanted to see her smile and laugh again. Yet, I sensed her sadness. I was sure she was sad because her male was a dishonorable coward and a weakling.

Angel suddenly rolled off the chair and stood, and I could smell the saltiness of her tears as she walked by. My heart sank in my chest. After a few seconds, I followed her.

She was in the hallway outside the bathroom toward the back of

Beast's castle when I caught her arm. She jerked to a stop and looked up at me with red-rimmed eyes.

"What is wrong?"

"Nothing."

Without thinking, I pulled her against me and almost smiled at the feeling of her round stomach pressing into me. Almost..."You are crying." I swiped at the moisture under her eyes.

She put her hands on my chest and pushed for a split second. Then her hands turned soft and caressing. "It's nothing."

"Do not lie to me." I lowered my face to hers and held her gaze. "You are sad. Please tell me why." Her gaze fell and she started to push away.

"Come." I pulled her into the bathroom and shut the door. I gave her a moment in which she took several deep breaths before I questioned her. "Are you sad because your male left you?"

"My—? Okay, first of all, it wasn't like that."

"What was it like?"

"The father of the baby didn't leave. Well, not the way you're thinking. Not voluntarily. He...he died."

It was then that I understood her tears. She was mourning her male. She had no one to care for her or her youngling. My heart ached. I had been such a fool to show her my anger. I was responsible for bringing these tears to her eyes. I looked skyward and ran my hand through my hair. When I turned to apologize, my arms once again wrapped themselves around her and to my surprise, she melted against me.

It was not mere pity I was feeling for her. Not at all. The kiss, however, was meant to comfort her. A simple brush of my lips to her forehead. Then her cheek. Her lips. As soon as our lips touched, I felt like I'd been punched in the chest. Heat shot to my extremities. My dragon roared to life as I held her firmly against me. She opened to me and I explored her mouth, savoring her, her taste exploding on my tongue.

Angel writhed in my arms and stroked her hands around to my back, digging her fingers into me harder and then moaning into my kiss. One of my hands tangled in her short curls.

Then, suddenly, it was over. She pushed against me and instead of desire coursing through her eyes, I saw anger. She took a couple steps back

"Stop it. Stop. This is not okay." She crossed her arms over her chest and glared.

I frowned and tried to move toward her, but again, she pushed me back. "What are you talking about?"

"What kind of person pretends to be attracted to a pregnant lady. What kind of sick joke is that? I know that you're just fucking with me and it's not okay." Again, I stepped forward and this time when she pushed me back, I caught her arm and dragged her into my chest. Holding her there, I lowered my mouth to her ear.

"I am not fucking with you. I would *like* to fuck with you. But that will be your choice. I do not wish to cause you discomfort or anger."

Then, before I could stop her, she pulled away from me and backed up until her back hit the wall on the opposite side of the bathroom. When I moved toward her, she held up her hands and worked to catch her breath.

I frowned. "My desire for you is no joke."

"Men like you didn't throw themselves at me when I wasn't eight and a half months pregnant. No way it's happening now."

She tilted her head and narrowed her eyes. "You're insane. That's it. You're insane and I just made out with you. Great. I just made out with a crazy person."

I was off balance and when she pushed past me. I stumbled into the sink and missed my chance to catch her. Before I could do anything, she scurried by and was back in the kitchen with everyone.

My dragon demanded I go and get Angel. It was not a good idea, though. She did not desire me and I'd angered her. I'd been playing with fire, anyway. I could not explain the connection I felt to her or the extreme need I had to protect her. She wasn't my mate. She would never be the female for me, no matter how much I wanted her to be, and I wanted her with everything in me.

I could hear her asking Beast to take her home and I stayed where I was, leaning over the bathroom counter, my hands gripping the polished granite. I stood there, staring at my reflection in the mirror, watching my dragon war with me to get out.

Chapter Ten

ANGEL

Labor began early Tuesday morning. I wasn't ready but the baby didn't care; she was. Around midafternoon, when the contractions were seven minutes apart, I used the app on my phone to order an Uber to transport me to Lafourche General.

The day was overcast and muggy as all get out. Looping the strap of my hospital bag over my shoulder, I headed out front to the wrap-around porch to wait for my ride to the hospital. One hand rested underneath my belly, supporting it. With the other, I clung to the infant car seat that I'd need to bring home Baby Girl.

I was terrified. Not so much of the giving-birth part—I'd read books about that and had a good idea of what was going to happen. I was terrified that somehow Baby Girl wouldn't make it, that she'd have some terrible illness or genetic condition or that the delivery would go awry and she'd be another in a long line of casualties whose only crime was they'd been associated with Angel of Death.

The Uber driver turned out to be an older man named Cecil who was sweet as pie. Thank god he didn't recognize me. If I thought Cecil would freak as soon as he saw my condition, I was wrong. The second he laid eyes on my ginormous belly, a big grin spread across his weathered face and he nodded knowingly. Before I could get in, he was out of the car and helping me into the backseat.

"Y'all just relax and keep breathin'. I'll git ya' to the General in time. Trust ol' Cecil."

Apparently, ol' Cecil thought that if he didn't remind me, I'd forget to breathe.

"This your first?"

I nodded and was about to reply when a major contraction struck and I grunted in pain.

"Breathe, honey, breathe."

Okay, I got what Cecil meant. Holy crap, labor pains were no joke.

"My wife and me, we got eleven babies and twenty-three grandbabies."

"Twenty thhhhh..." Another contraction hit. They were speeding up exponentially. Was it even possible to breathe through these things? I found myself panting, but I couldn't get in a deep breath until it was over.

"Your wife went through this eleven times and didn't castrate you? What was she thinking? I'd have gotten out the sewing sheers after the third or fourth."

Cecil laughed heartily. "I know it seems that way now, but just you wait until you holdin' that lil' bundle o' joy in yer arms. You'll see. Ain't nothin' else like it."

He shook his head emphatically as I *breathed* through another contraction. "No, sir, nothin' at all."

As soon as we pulled up to the hospital, I was plopped into a wheel chair, midcontraction, and carted off to the maternity ward. I had little brain power with which to worry. Giving birth was the most painful thing I've ever gone through. Like having my internal organs pulled out through my vagina.

Baby Girl was born two hours later. Seven pounds, seven ounces, she came out with a head full of thick, black hair.

I didn't have a name for her. I hadn't planned on being the one to name her. That was not supposed to be my job. With pen rolling over the paper, I found myself filling out the name field on the birth certificate form the following day as *Mia Amelia Arceneaux*.

Mother: *Angel Arceneaux.*

Father: *unknown.*

I wanted to honor Amie and Jeremiah in some way and the name Mia Amelia seemed to do that.

Just as I finished filling out the form, the most upbeat nurse in the world entered my room. She was carrying a huge bouquet with one of those mylar balloons that said "baby." When she placed them on my night stand, I knew Nurse Cheerful had made a mistake.

"Those flowers aren't mine."

She frowned and removed the little florist card. "They say Angel Arceneaux on the card."

"Who are they from?"

"Doesn't say. Maybe the baby's father?"

"Definitely not the baby's father."

The nurse shrugged and winked. "Secret admirer then."

Secret admirer? I wondered if they might be from Sky. But, how would she know Mia had been born? Then a shudder came over me and my blood ran cold. Was it possible that they were from Amie's family? No, they couldn't possibly know either. Amie hadn't even told her coworkers about our "arrangement". How would they have found out? What if they did?

"I have good news." Nurse Cheerful smiled a megawatt smile that probably worked like a charm on most of her patients. "You and Mia are both healthy and can be discharged as soon as you have a ride home."

An hour later, Mia was dressed in a cute little newborn outfit and I was out of my hospital gown and wearing a pair of loose sweats. I shuffled around the room as I waited for a call from the front desk that my Uber had arrived. It never came. A huge, muscular hunk showed up instead.

"Armand? What are you doing here?" Not that I minded seeing him. In fact, he was dressed in dark, low-slung denims and a black T-shirt that strained to fit over his broad chest and bulging biceps. He was a sight for sore eyes, and I'm pretty sure he made quite a splash as he passed the nursing station.

"I have come to transport you and your youngling home."

"Youngli—my baby? Thanks, but no thanks. I called an Uber."

He scowled disapprovingly. "You will take a ride from a stranger rather than a friend? "

He had a point. "But I might get a bad review if I don't show."

"You will not. I paid him handsomely."

"You paid an Uber driver so you could take me home yourself?

He didn't answer. His eyes were glued to Mia. As I watched, he took a couple of steps forward and peeked into the bassinette. I suddenly had a sneaking suspicion. "Armand, are those flowers from you?"

Again, he didn't answer, but I knew I was right. "They are from you. Why? How did you know?"

"You deserve flowers. You have birthed a beautiful young...er, baby."

At that moment, Nurse Cheerful waltzed into the room with a wheelchair. "Alrighty, since your ride's here, I guess you're all set."

"Uh, I don't need that. I'm good to walk."

"Of course you are." Why did Nurse Cheerful have to say every-thing as though she was singing it? "But it's policy."

I tried to sing back, "No, thank you, I'll walk," but it emerged sounding as though I was an old man who'd swallowed a bullfrog. A singer, I was not.

"If you do not wish to ride in that chair with wheels, I will carry you."

"What about Mia?"

"I will carry you both."

I rolled my eyes, then gasped as he scooped me up in one arm as though it was no effort whatsoever. "See. You weigh nothing." Nurse Cheerful was giggling hysterically. I glowered at her, but she was too busy ogling Armand to notice.

"Put me the hell down! Okay, y'all win. I'll sit in the damned wheelchair."

———

When we reached Armand's truck, he opened the passenger door and

I looked up at up him. "Ugh, not sure how I'm gonna get into that thing." I looked back up at the truck, a raised Power Stroke turbo diesel. The damned thing looked like a monster truck. It was bad enough I was leaving Lafourche General in what amounted to adult diapers, but no way was I gonna stretch out my still-sore undercarriage by attempting to climb into the thing.

He wrapped his hands around my waist, lifted me, and placed me gently in the seat like I was featherweight glass. Then, he walked around to his side, and the three of us—me, Armand, and baby Mia in the infant car seat—were off.

I had to admit, it didn't feel half bad to have someone pick me up from the hospital. Someone who just wanted to do it, rather than being paid to. An Uber would have sufficed. It was what I was used to —taking care of myself, making my own arrangements. But it felt good to have someone show up for me. And Mia. I wondered what it would be like to have someone like Armand around all the time. Not someone *like* Armand—Armand.

When we arrived at my home, Armand offered to walk me inside and get settled, but I steadfastly refused. He respected my wishes and didn't push to come inside, but he did insist on walking me and Mia to the ; he stood on the porch and watched as we entered.

Once Mia was settled in her bassinette, I wandered over to the nursery window and was surprised to see Armand's truck still in my driveway.

As cynical and pessimistic as I tended to be, I had to admit, Armand was a special guy. He was going to make some woman a great husband someday. Not me though. I wouldn't do that to him. No man survived me.

We stayed like that for a long time—me looking out the window, him behind the wheel—until he finally restarted the engine and drove away.

Chapter Eleven

ANGEL

The first week was hell. I barely slept, Mia screamed nonstop, my nipples were sore and cracked, and Mia didn't take well to breastfeeding. Maybe because she knew she didn't belong to me. Whenever I looked at her, I felt guilty. To top it off, on the rare occasions I did steal some shut-eye, I had nightmares of zombie-like creatures trying to tear Mia from my arms as they chanted, "She's ours... She's ours." Every time it happened, I woke up covered in sweat and breastmilk.

The second week was a little better. The nightmares persisted but were less frequent, and Mia learned to latch on better. As a result, her belly was fuller, she slept for longer stretches and my nipples healed. I felt a little less like I'd kidnapped someone's baby.

The third week, I was ready to show Mia the world. I was apprehensive about going out with her, for fear of zombies snatching her—or, Amie's family snatching her. Or anyone knowing I was an imposter.

I knew what the right thing to do was. And I tried to convince myself to do it. Daily, I tried. I wanted sweet Mia to have the best. She deserved to grow up in a loving two-parent home surrounded by friends and family. Not a mausoleum with a weird, cursed goth chick.

Since Jeremiah had no family, all decisions about Mia's future should have defaulted to Amie's family.

When I looked down at the cute little bundle—when she looked back at me with those big, wide eyes full of contentment and wonder, I couldn't do it. Not yet. I at least needed to breastfeed her for the first few months of her life. They said breastmilk was best and, although we'd had a rough start, Mia and I had just gotten the hang of it.

And she reached for me. When she slept, she liked to hold my finger.

I was so conflicted. I had a cloud of darkness over me that never failed to touch those around me. I couldn't doom her to that. No, I couldn't keep her. When she held my finger, though, she was my heart. I didn't know how I would ever let her go.

But I had to...

My curse had started when I was seven. My parents died in a horrific airplane crash. There was never any conclusive evidence to explain why the plane crashed and the wreckage went up in a fiery inferno.

After that, I went to live with my Grandma Gertie, a sweet old woman who doted on me. I adored her. But a week later, she fell down the stairs in her home and died a few days after that.

My great-uncle Elias took me in next and I was pretty sure the only reason he lived as long as he did was because he avoided me as much as possible. He remained distant and cold, and I barely saw him. He was away on business a lot and left me to be raised either by housekeepers when I was small or, in later years, just by myself.

A few months after I turned nineteen, Uncle Elias was leaving on a business meeting in downtown New Orleans when a sudden thunderstorm kicked up. Not really unusual for NOLA, but as he ran to his car, he was hit by a bolt of lightning—struck dead in his tracks.

Even my first crush in third grade, Jimmy Henderson, who held my hand on the way home from school and one time pulled me behind the bushes so we could sneak our first kiss, died from a snake bite. True, it wasn't until years later when I was in college and hadn't even seen him for a decade, but still, dead is dead.

My prom date was killed by a drunk driver days before graduation. The guy I met at my first college mixer, developed a rare, exotic, and deadly disease while on a mission trip to Bora Bora. And then there was Alan Dougerson.

Alan was a charmer. He was a man who was hard to resist. He was handsome, outgoing, the life of the party. I was a weird, lonely wall-flower-type chick with no family and lots of money who was completely fooled by him. I had no idea he was an addict and a cheater. No idea he already had a girlfriend and was just dating me to gain my trust so he could rob me blind.

He didn't get away with it, though. As soon as I noticed the safe open and the silverware gone, I called the cops and reported him. Turned out he already had a rap sheet a mile long. Then, eight days later, he was involved in a high-speed car chase, took a mountain turn too fast, and careened his sports car right off the edge of a cliff.

Because of the police report, the press got hold of the story, and some ambitious junior reporter started digging into my past. That was when I, the victim, became, in the court of public opinion, the perpetrator.

The reporter probably thought he was being clever and funny finding out that so many people in my life had died and labeling me Angel of Death. It wasn't funny to me. It turned my life into a circus and me into some spectacle. People taunted me, jeered at me, I even received death threats. There were some, like Amie and Jeremiah, who didn't believe in the curse. Amie and Jeremiah almost had me convinced it was all ridiculous nonsense...until they, too, died.

As I loaded Mia into her stroller, I readied myself to face the world. I would figure out the best course of action and the best timing to implement it. I just needed sunshine, fresh air, and to get off the property. A long walk would do us both good and allow me to think clearly, outside of the safe cocoon of my walled mansion and secluded estate.

Chapter Twelve

ANGEL

As usual, there was a pile of gifts, like offerings, placed at my front door. This time, there were three boxes of diapers, four giant stuffed animals, a Dora the Explorer backpack, and a stack of Disney DVDs.

In the past, I'd found receiving blankets, baby swings, car seats, diaper bags, clothes in sizes from newborn to 6T, teething rings, toys, rocking chairs, and yesterday there was a stack of college brochures.

It wasn't just one of each thing either. I had enough "anonymous" gifts to start my own Babies R Us. I was pretty sure I knew who was leaving them, I just didn't know why.

I shoveled the gifts into the foyer and maneuvered the stroller—another gift left at my doorstep—out onto the wraparound porch.

As I wheeled Mia down the walkway toward the small door in the wall surrounding the estate, I stopped a moment to scan the sky. Lately, the cleaning women from the maid service and the groundskeepers both mentioned seeing an unusually large bird or a small plane—they weren't sure which—flying the skies around the estate. Probably just a hawk or an eagle.

The walk from my home into town was only about a half mile, and the fresh air and sunshine were already doing both Mia and me some good. While Mia cooed in her stroller, I inhaled deeply. I assumed I was still persona non grata in town due to my death curse, so I wore oversized, dark sunglasses and a headscarf and looked a little like a 1950's starlet.

I strolled through the square, pushing Mia on the busy Friday morning, window shopping and appreciating the bright sunshine. As we passed the town's little movie theater, the scent of buttered popcorn wafted from the darkened doorway.

I smiled down at Mia who, if her kicking and cooing was any indication, was enjoying her first outing immensely. "Do you smell that? If you take after me, you'll fall in love with popcorn. When you're old enough to try it, that is." Of course, there would be no reason for her to take after me. We didn't even share the same DNA.

I inhaled one more lungful of popcorn-scented air and then started across the street to Notions and Whatnots, the little novelty store. Before I got halfway across, though, I saw his reflection in the shop window. Armand.

He was strolling casually but purposefully behind me as though he was...following me? I swung around. It was Armand all right. He was dressed not unlike the last time I'd seen him, in a tight T-shirt and dark-blue jeans. His footsteps ate up the ground between us until he was standing in front of me. "Angel."

I pursed my lips and white-knuckled the stroller handlebar. I wanted to reach up and adjust the headscarf I was wearing. I wanted to smooth down my shirt, or run home and change out of my yoga pants. I hadn't even put on makeup. I gripped the stroller and forced a light smile. "Armand. Good to see you again."

He smiled and I was totally unprepared for the goosebumps that instantly exploded all over my body.

He peered down into the stroller and smiled broadly at Mia who seemed to be entranced by him. Then he looked back at me. "It is good to see you. Both."

We stood staring into each other's eyes, and for a split second, I felt as though I could almost read his thoughts—.

A horn honking brought me back to reality. I jumped and then noticed we were still standing in the middle of the street, so I propelled Mia's stroller up and over the curb.

Once safely on the sidewalk, I thought to ask Armand about the gifts that I was sure he was leaving on my porch. They had to be from him, and he'd spent a small fortune. But before I could open my mouth to speak, my empty stomach rumbled loudly. Nice.

"You are hungry?"

I smiled sheepishly. "I skipped breakfast and I guess the time's gotten away from me. I hadn't realized it was past lunchtime."

The look that crossed over Armand's face made me think for a moment that he was going to scold me like a child. Then his features softened. "Please allow me to take you to lunch."

The man looked so hopeful, I couldn't say no. Not that I wanted to. I mean, it's not every day I get asked to lunch by a man who could easily grace the cover of a romance novel.

As Armand led me to the nearest diner, his hand rested against my lower back. The gesture felt too intimate, but I didn't want him to move it.

I slipped inside the diner ahead of Armand and a hostess scurried to the front holding menus in her hand and forcing a tight smile. Even though I was still wearing my headscarf and big glasses, for a moment I wondered if she recognized me. Then her eyes landed on Armand. Her smile broadened so wide I thought her face might crack and I would swear her eyelashes started fluttering.

I cleared my throat to get her attention. "Something in your eye?"

She scowled but didn't answer; instead, she spun on her heel. "Follow me." She led us to a small table in the back. Mia's stroller was a tight fit, but I managed to only bump into a couple of tables on the way.

I became a little apprehensive about being seen with Armand. As it was my first time back out in public since having Mia, I felt like everyone was watching , and I was suddenly worried about someone shouting something about me being the Angel of Death. The thought of Armand witnessing that and judging me through that lens made me cringe.

Once we were seated, Armand scooted his chair closer to mine and then smiled down at Mia in her stroller. "Can I hold her?"

I was a little taken aback by the request, and I took a second to reply. "Um... yeah, sure."

Wide-eyed, Mia didn't have a care in the world as I picked her up and handed her to Armand. He was extra careful with her, holding her like she was made of spun sugar, as he brought her to his chest and held her there. His big hands made her body look minuscule, but they were so tender and gentle.

Seeing him hold her did something to me. It started neurons firing in my brain that had no business firing. I remembered the kiss we'd shared in Beast and Sky's bathroom. I wondered if he would ever wanted to kiss me again. Had he enjoyed it as much as I had? Little butterflies fluttered straight to my core as I remembered the feeling of being wrapped in his arms. Suddenly, I wanted him with an urgency that I didn't understand.

His eyes snapped up to mine, and I watched as he inhaled deeply through his nose. His purple eyes shone brightly. He leaned in towards me. "You are staring at me, Angel."

I licked my lips, an unconscious action that drew his eyes down to my mouth. "You're staring back."

The small coo from Mia broke up the sexual tension between us and I looked down at her to find her staring up at Armand, her eyes almost glossy with joy. I chuckled at the fact that she seemed to find Armand just as irresistible as I did.

"I think she likes me."

"She does like you. She doesn't drool like that for just anyone." I pulled a towel out of my bag and leaned over to wipe Mia's mouth.

"You can put her back if you want."

"She's fine. She barely weighs anything."

"Easy for you to say. You have all those muscles on top of muscles and stuff..." I bit my lip and looked away. Why did I say that? My mind scrambled for another topic to change the subject, which was currently his muscles. "So, it's funny running into you like this. Do you live around here or something?"

"No, I don't. I was picking something up from a store close by when I saw you."

"Yeah, speaking of stores. Mia and I seem to have a benevolent gift giver. You wouldn't know anything about that, would you?"

He didn't cop to it, but he did grin. "You deserve gifts. Both of you."

I laughed. "I knew it was you! Thank you. From both of us. But I have enough toys and diapers and stuff to open my own baby boutique. I'm going to have to donate two thirds of the stuff to charity. Not that I'm not grateful—I am—but, it needs to stop. And what's with the college brochures?"

"It is never too early to start planning for college."

I couldn't help laughing at that. Armand's eyes seemed to light up as he watched my response. "I will stop on one condition."

"Okay, I'm listening."

"I will stop if you agree to have lunch with me again."

"How about next Tuesday? Okay?"

"Okay."

After our food arrived, we ate in silence, with Armand holding little Mia in one arm while he ate with the other. She contented herself with watching him outright, while I tried to be more discrete about it. When she got fussy, he rocked her into a nap. Still, he held her.

I couldn't help but think what a good father Armand would be.

Chapter Thirteen

ARMAND

"S-sir, excuse me, but you're scaring away our customers. M-maybe you can pace back and forth in front of the florists? Or the shoe store?"

I turned to stare at the small human male speaking to me. His name was pinned to his chest. Manny. Short and slender, he was trembling slightly as he leaned his head out of the café using the door to shield the rest of him.

"I-it's just that it's time for our lunch rush, and people are scared to come in because you're pacing out here and making that...*sound*."

Sound? The growl I was emitting was involuntary. I was frantic. Angel and Mia and I had been meeting for lunch every Tuesday and Friday at noon for the last three weeks. Tuesdays, we met at Beau's Diner for po'boys, and Fridays, it was Cayenne Café. It was twenty minutes past noon on a Friday and no Angel.

Just as I was about to turn to the little man and bite his ugly head from his scrawny neck, Angel rounded the corner, pushing Mia in the stroller. Thank the stars! I reached her side in three strides and gathered her into my arms.

"Ahh! Ouch, Armand, you're squeezing me!"

I loosened my grip, but I could not release her yet. "Where were you? I was afraid something had happened to you? I was beside myself! If anything happened, I would never forgive—"

"You're also shouting and making a scene." She wriggled loose from my grasp. "Can we talk about this inside?" Angel's cheeks were flushed, and she looked around at the heads that were turned in our direction.

I did not care that onlookers gawked. Let them stare. If they had no business of their own to mind, they were sorry and pitiful, and their opinions mattered very little to me anyway. I did not care what they thought or how they felt. But I did care how Angel felt. So, I quieted and ushered her and Mia inside the café.

As Angel lifted a squirming, cooing Mia from the stroller, I folded the apparatus and stored it in the corner of the establishment, and we were seated at our regular corner table.

"Can I get y'all something to drink?" A waiter stopped beside Angel and smiled at us. There was nothing in the man's eyes that said he was thinking about Angel in any way but friendly, yet I found myself wanting to snap him in half.

"A sweet tea, please. And then I'll have the special." Angel looked at me, and her long eyelashes fluttered.

"Same for me."

As soon as he was gone, Angel leaned in closer. "I'm going to run to the ladies' room. Keep an eye on Mia for me."

As I nodded, she placed the tiny, squirmy youngling in my arms, and as I smiled down at her, my heart melted as it usually did. She waved her tiny arms and blew saliva bubbles.

I laughed. "Good girl. Very impressive."

Where have you been, brother? I've been looking all over for you. Ovide's thoughts invaded my head.

I have been...around.

I have checked every bar in a twenty-mile radius of your home the past week.

I wasn't sure I wanted to tell him that I had not been to a bar since I'd met Angel. My quest for a mate had been put on hold. I had been spending every night for the past six weeks perched on Angel's roof, watching over her and Mia.

I have been busy.

Busy doing what?

Things.

There was a long pause during which Ovide waited for me to say more, but I refused.

I see.

I stared down at the little bundle of sunshine in my arms. She was the most beautiful youngling that had ever been born. And right then, as I watched her, she gave me a toothless, gummy little grin. *She smiled! She smiled at me!*

Who—what? Who smiled at you?

The youngling, Mia, her first smile!

What youngling? Whose youngling?

Never mind. Let yourself in and take all the brew you want. I am too busy to be bothered, Ovide.

Alright, bro, alright. I just hope you know what you're doing.

My heart was full to bursting. I knew Ovide would have thought I'd lost my mind spending my time with a human female and her young rather than continuing the quest for my own mate, but truly, in that moment, I was resigned to the fact that I would never find a mate. I no longer believed it was in the cards for me because, once a dragon found his mate, his entire world revolved around her. Beast, Cezar, Blaise, and Remy were a testament to that fact. They would kill and die for their mates. Without their mates, they would cease to exist. For me, that was not so. I was certain in that moment that there was no female that I could ever care more about—no female that I would ever place above Mia and Angel.

"I can take her back now if you want." Angel plopped into the seat across from me and spread her napkin across her lap.

I didn't want to. I wanted to hold the little sweetie in my arms for as long as I could. "She smiled at me." I could not have been prouder.

"She did? It's her new trick to endear people to her, and it works like a charm, doesn't it? I'm sorry I was late today, by the way. I had a doctor's appointment, and it ran over.

A chill ran through me. "Doctor? Are you ill?" Was I not looking out for her well enough? The thought of Angel not being healthy made my stomach turn.

"No, silly. It was just a six-week checkup with my OB/GYN."

I tried to sound out the letters. "Oh-bee-gein? What is an oh-bee-gein doctor?"

"O-B-G-Y-N. It stands for obstetrician-gynecologist. It's a doctor that delivers babies and examines female parts. You know, to make sure everything is good down there after squeezing something the size of a watermelon out an opening the size of a grape."

"Is everything okay with your opening?"

She barked out a laugh. "Yes. I'm all healed, and I was given the A-okay to resume sexual activity."

I was midsip of my sweet tea when Angel spoke the word *sexual*. My throat clenched and shot sweet tea back out the way it came.

The waiter, who chose that moment to deliver our sandwiches, didn't hide a chuckle very well, but I let it slide because he quickly brought a stack of paper napkins to clean the mess.

Angel giggled wickedly. "Sorry, didn't mean to make you choke."

I did not believe that for a second. The little minx knew exactly what she was doing.

Suddenly, my eyes narrowed. "Is there someone you are planning to have sexual activity with?"

"Well, I wouldn't use the word planning."

"What word would you use?"

"Wishing? Hoping?" Angel's voice had grown huskier. Still holding little Mia to my chest, I raised my eyes to meet her mother's and felt my world shift when her eyebrow lifted in a silent challenge.

I squirmed to adjust myself beneath the table. It made no sense, I shouldn't have felt anything for Angel, the same way I'd felt nothing for any of the hundreds of other women I'd met who were also not my mate. But I did. Not only did I feel something for her, I felt everything for her. The mere thought of Angel lying with another male sent me into a rage.

I wanted desperately for her to be mine—to claim her. I knew it didn't work that way, but I couldn't convince my mind or my dragon otherwise. And, mate or not, I wanted to accept her implied invitation. I longed to hold her in my arms and pleasure her to find every sensitive place on her body and devote myself to tasting and teasing until she screamed out my name.

There was one big thing stopping me. I did not want to hurt Angel. What if I did meet my mate? What then? I could not just have sex with Angel and then leave her for another. I would not hurt her that way. It would kill me to cause her pain.

It was a difficult decision to make and even more difficult to try to explain to her the reason I had for rejecting her offer. As I searched for the words to explain, she said something that changed the direction of my thoughts.

"Only on one condition, though. And it's nonnegotiable."

"What condition is that?"

She leaned forward conspiratorially. "No strings. I don't do relationships. It's straight up sex with no attachment or nothing."

A smile spread across my face, and I nodded. "No strings."

"Great!" She sat back and waggled her eyebrows at me. "How'd you like a tour of my home?"

I raised my hand to flag down our waiter. "We will take our check now, please."

We left our food untouched.

Chapter Fourteen

ANGEL

I'd eased Mia back into her stroller on our walk to my home. The timing was perfect because, by the time we arrived back at my house, it would be her nap time. That meant Armand and I could be alone. There was something boiling between us, something so intense that I could feel the electricity flowing between us.

I stopped at the little door hidden in the brick wall, half grown over with vines and budding , and slipped the key in. Pushing it open, I led us through. The experience was always kind of magical. When I was younger, I used to pretend it was my own secret garden.

I could barely believe what I was about to do. I was about to do the deed with the sexiest, kindest man I'd ever met. Not only was Armand tall, well-built and gorgeous, he was charming. The walls I'd constructed against men like my exes weren't prepared to withstand a man like Armand. The funny, caring and sweet man created a constant fire in my belly.

I couldn't let myself get too into him, though. Doing so would risk his life. Whatever went on between us had to stay strictly platonic—friends with benefits. I knew I couldn't bear it if Armand became yet another casualty of Angel of Death.

Once inside, he held the sleeping Mia as I led us up the grand staircase to Mia's nursery. He placed her gently in her bassinette and we both smiled down at her.

Eyes still on Mia, Armand's hand reached for mine and for several minutes, we stayed like that, hands clasped, eyes on the sleeping infant.

"Are we on the same page, Armand?"

He cleared his throat. "What page is that?"

Not able to look at him while I said it, I kept my eyes on the bassinette. "The page where there's sex with no strings."

"Ah, that page." A pause followed.

"Armand, I can't...I can't attach myself to anyone."

He grunted. "I understand."

"Is that a problem?"

"It is not a problem."

He turned and stared down at me, a storm brewing behind those deep purple eyes. His mouth pressed into a thin line as he stroked his fingers over the stubble on his jaw. "No attachments. Just sex."

I nodded, feeling that same storm swirling within me. I hated hearing the words, for whatever stupid reason. But they had to be said.

He stepped closer, his chest close enough that a deep inhale would've made my nipples brush against him.

The heated look in his eyes turned my knees to jelly. I licked my lips and swiped the baby monitor from the nightstand. "I need to hear if she cries." I turned on the monitor and slowly backed away from the bassinette and Armand.

I stopped when my back hit the doorway out of the room. When my eyes met Armand's, I could have sworn I saw flames dancing in his pupils. Our eyes remained locked as I backed out of the room reaching down to catch the hem of my shirt. Armand followed me, never closing the distance, just watching and following. I pulled my shirt over my head and dropped it at my feet in the hallway.

I had a fleeting moment of shyness about my postpregnancy body which was swallowed up by the fiery passion in Armand's eyes as his gaze raked over every inch of me. He regarded me as though I was the most breathtaking sight he'd ever seen. Boy, if that didn't make a girl feel beautiful.

I backed into my bedroom, the room with sweeping views of the swamp that I'd explored as a girl. Unhooking my bra, I turned to find Armand leaning against the doorway, watching with hooded eyes.

I let the material slide away and then bent to step out of my pants. In just my underwear, I straightened to find Armand inches behind me. "Tell me now that you want this, Angel. I want you to be sure."

I looked up at him, my bottom lip caught between my teeth. There was nothing I wanted more at that moment. I reached up and wrapped my arms around his neck pressing my breasts against his chest. The contact sent electric currents flowing through my hyperaware body and I gasped. "Oh, I want this."

Chapter Fifteen

ARMAND

Angel was enchanting. I followed her, caught in her spell as she removed her clothing piece by piece to slowly reveal her exquisite feminine form.

Her hips swayed as she walked, a titillating dance that left my mouth watering. When she turned to me and said those three words, "I want this," I knew I was the luckiest, most honored dragon that ever existed.

I reached out and with my fingertips, gently explored the soft, jiggling flesh of her breast. As I teased her puckered nipple, she moaned softly and arched her back slightly. When a small droplet of milk fell from her nipple, she gasped and searched my face for a reaction.

I leaned down and used the tip of my tongue to lick the droplet off. She moaned, encouraging me to drag my tongue over her nipple in teasing circles. Her soft panting affected me so much, my cock was already ready to explode.

Wanting nothing more than to continue pleasuring her, I reached my hand between her thighs and gently stroked her over her already damp panties. I wanted to wring more of her soft moans from her lips.

I slipped a finger underneath the cotton and along her wet folds.

Angel gasped and her skin flushed, her arousal perfuming the room with the most delicious aroma I had ever smelled.

She was hot and wet, and I was overcome with the need to taste her, to pleasure her with my mouth. I scooped her up and carried her to the bed, placing her gently in the middle.

Peppering kisses down her stomach, I removed the undergarment. Amidst her gasps and cries of pleasure, I flicked my tongue over her sweet folds until she writhed against the bedding. As the volume of her moans increased, I pushed a finger deep inside. When she cried out my name, I struggled to maintain my control.

I did not want to lose my seed too early, but without even being touched, I was right on the edge. I stroked her with my fingers as my mouth remained on her, my tongue making love to her.

As I felt her shuddering trembles, I raised up to see her head thrown back, her lips parted, and her cheeks pink, and I knew she was close. Slowly, I slid my engorged cock into her as she dug her fingers into my back.

Slowly, agonizingly slowly, I slid into and out of Angel, rocking against her.

"Armand..." Angel's voice broke as she called out to me, her body spasming around me as she trembled with her release.

I rocked against her once more, but with the clamp of her body around my shaft, I could no longer hold back. I released my own climax into the female beneath me.

For a long time, we remained with her clutched around me so tightly that it was almost painful as I battled my dragon to keep from marking her. But, mark or no mark, I could not help feeling that forevermore, Angel had claimed my soul.

Angel

Two weeks later...

. . .

Sex with Armand was a drug. I wanted more even while I was still just coming down from the last high. I didn't know the rules that went along with sleeping with a man casually. I didn't know the rules of sleeping with a man at all. Was multiple times a night normal? Was I normal? I felt like I'd just been reborn a sex addict.

For two weeks, Armand arrived every night and we not only had mind-blowing sex, but he held me in his arms until morning. I made him leave before sunup when I got up for Mia's morning feeding. I got the feeling the only reason he didn't stick around longer was because I forced him to go.

When I was awakened by Mia's gentle fussing through the baby monitor, I unwrapped myself from Armand and slipped out of bed. I pulled my pink chenille bathrobe around my sore but satiated body and hurried to the room next door, her nursery.

She wasn't fully awake quite yet, just stirring, readying for her morning nursing. I moved to her bassinette and scooped her into my arms. She had no idea of the storm her mother had stirred up. But, no matter how much I claimed that the sex would be no strings, I felt strings. I felt big, messy strings.

"You are incredible."

I spun around to find Armand standing in the doorway, the look in his eyes was one of utter devotion and it scared the bejesus out of me.

Chapter Sixteen

ARMAND

"I know you're sleeping with Angel. I want to know what the hell you think you're doing." Sky's arms were crossed over her chest, and she was frowning deeply.

"She told you?" Angel had been adamant about keeping everything we did together , and the fact that she may have talked to Sky about it surprised me.

"No, I haven't seen her since she had the baby. Beast told me. He can smell her scent on you."

For some reason, this revelation thrilled me. Mates almost always carried the scent of their other half. It was a way to let those whose senses were refined enough to detect it—those who carried animals inside—know that you were unavailable. The shifter equivalent of a human wedding ring. Although Angel and I would never have a true claiming, I loved that I carried her scent.

"We are simply...enjoying ourselves right now." For fire's sake, I didn't know what the hell I was doing with her. I only knew that when I was with her I felt alive in ways I'd never experienced before. I knew that the mere thought of not being around for Angel and Mia if they needed anything twisted my gut into knots. I couldn't stay away from them.

"I know it's none of my business what two consenting adults do, but that girl's been through a lot. She's endured a lot of bullying and people have not been kind to her. I just don't want to see her hurt when you suddenly find your mate and dump her like a hot potato you can't get rid of fast enough."

My dragon suddenly sat up and took notice. "What do you mean bullying? Who has bullied her? Tell me and I will destroy them!"

"Whoa there, big guy. It's a long story that I don't want to get into with you. Besides, it's hers to tell. The point is, you're not being fair to her and you know that."

Everything Sky was saying, I had already considered. I was stuck in a conundrum. I could not claim her and I could not leave her. It would gut me to see Angel or Mia hurt. I would cut off my left wing before I would intentionally inflict pain on either one of them. I rolled my neck and tried to ease the sudden tension from my shoulders.

"The arrangement was her idea. She was adamant about having no strings. She insisted I agree to it. "

Throwing her hands up, Sky spoke to her kitchen ceiling. "Lord 'a mercy, save me from clueless dragons." Then she looked me straight in the eye. "Women never mean that! There are always strings. Always."

Sky had a point and I had hoped Angel had developed strings. While I knew the eclipse was coming and none of us were sure exactly how long after the event it would take, we did know that an unmated adult male dragon would begin a rapid deterioration into insanity. I was willing to accept that as my fate as long as it meant I could spend what little time I had remaining with Angel and Mia.

"I understand. I will take care of it, Sky. I will not treat Angel like a potato." I rose from the bar stool and made my way to the door, full of resolve. I would lay all my cards on the table with Angel that evening. Everything. I would show her my dragon. I would tell her my time was limited. I would tell her that I wanted to spend every last moment of my life with her.

"Thank you, Armand. I knew you would listen to reason. Good luck with the mate hunt."

I merely grunted.

As I stepped out onto Beast's dock, I considered the words I would use to explain the dragon. Should I show her first or should I discuss it, describe it, and then show her?

"Don't make us do it, brother." Beast's voice came from the shadow cast by the afternoon sun. I snapped my head in his direction.

I had been so immersed in my thoughts I had not realized he was sitting in his favorite comfortable patio chair. "I did not notice you there."

"She's not your mate."

I growled angrily. "It is my business."

"It is not. It is the business of all of us if we are tasked with the undertaking of putting you down." Beast slammed his fist on the armrest of his chair so hard it cracked in half, fell off the chair and dropped to the patio floor. He growled. "Blazing scales I loved that chair."

I slumped down onto the ottoman in front of him. I desperately wanted to argue with him but I was lacking ammunition.

"It cannot work, Armand. Even if you like her enough to pretend that she's your mate, it won't end well. What happens when the eclipse arrives and you haven't truly mated? You lose your mind and maybe you go down easy. What if you don't, though? What if you lose yourself and hurt her? What if you hurt that youngling?"

I shot up so fast, the ottoman fell backward onto its side. "I will end myself before I hurt either one of them."

"Just promise to keep looking for your mate. That's all I ask, just keep looking. You do not understand what it would do to us to have to battle and destroy you." Beast's head hung low as he shook it, lost in some vision. Perhaps it was a vision of our exodus from our native world and the horrors of the slaughter the dragon slayers wrought among our kind.

Seeing him like that consumed me with guilt. We were warriors, but even as warriors, we'd seen more horrors than any soldier should. The slaughter of our families, our friends, our homes—all that we knew desecrated and destroyed. How selfish I was to ask my fellow brethren to destroy me because I had chosen to give up the quest for a mate.

When Beast spoke, I was surprised to hear his voice quaver with emotion. "Promise."

The silence stretched before us. Finally, when I could no longer stand it, I responded. "Yes, yes, I promise."

I did not remain there. Taking to the air, I flew high and fast. I wanted to get far away from Sky and Beast and their perfect, blissful union.

I let out an angry roar as Beast's words sank in. Flying higher and higher, I let the sun's heat burn hot on my back. I flew up until I couldn't drag in a breath anymore in the thin air. I did not want for Beast to be right.

I hated the thought of having a female in my arms who was not Angel. I wanted only her.

At what cost, though? Would I be hurting both her and my brethren in the long run? The answer was out of my grasp.

But I had made a promise to Beast, and I did not take my promises lightly. I hated the thought of going back to frequenting bars and mingling with other females. I absolutely despised it.

Yet, I would compromise. I would stop in and drink the human urine-tasting beverage. If a female approached me, I would determine whether or not she was my mate, then I would leave and spend the rest of the night where I desperately wanted to be—with my Angel.

Chapter Seventeen

ANGEL

It'd been weeks since I'd visited Bon Temps Café. I had avoided it because of the memories the place harbored for me, but the excited look on Sky's face when I walked in told me that I'd been missed.

She rushed over, leaving her table in the middle of taking their order. She wrapped her arms around me, pulling me into a tight hug before bending down to peek at Mia. "Oh, Angel. She's beautiful! A sweet little doll baby. What's her name?"

"Mia. Mia Amelia."

Her eyes snapped up to mine and she let out a little breath. I wasn't sure if she'd catch on that I'd chosen the name because it closely mimicked Jeremiah and Amie's names, but her response removed any doubt. Tears filled her eyes. "Oh, Angel."

Sky led me over to a booth in the corner. "I have a break coming up in five minutes. Just let me get this order in, and I'll come visit with you."

I pulled Mia from her stroller and slid into the booth. Mia looked around the diner with wide, curious eyes, observing everything. She was as smart as a whip already. Her little fingers found their way into her mouth and drool spilled out. A loud hiccup preceded more drool.

Sky slid into the booth a few minutes later. "Look at her. I can't get over how beautiful she is. And how much hair she has! Cherry's daughter, Molly, is still as bald as can be." She looked longingly at Mia until I held Mia out for her. "Are you sure?"

Once Mia was in her arms, I sat back and watched Sky hold her. She stared down at her like Mia was the perfect baby. And she was.

Finally, Sky looked up and met my eyes. "I have so many questions and I know that none of them are my business, but they're beating around in my head like crazy."

I looked away, knowing already that she wanted to know about my relationship with Amie and Jeremiah. Perhaps she suspected the truth. "I'm...I'm not ready to talk about all of it. I'm still making up my mind about some stuff."

Her brows furrowed, but she nodded. "Maybe later."

I stayed quiet for a moment, thinking about what she'd want to know. What did she suspect? Hell, maybe she just wanted to ask me why I live alone in a huge antebellum mansion. Or not.

Regardless of the questions, I was terrified to start revealing things. If it slipped that Mia wasn't really mine...

I knew what I was doing wasn't right. But it felt so right. I wasn't sure I could handle her being taken from me. Even though that was what should've happened. I was tremendously selfish. She deserved to be with someone else. Yet, I couldn't seem to let go of her. Much like I couldn't seem to let go of Armand. My selfishness had hit maximum overload.

"You've birthed a beautiful baby, Angel. Good job! She's magnificent. I bet *you* could use a break, you know, from being Mommy—just for a night."

I felt my face burn bright. "I've been okay."

"I still think a night away would do you good. To remind you that you're not just a mom. You're still you. I know, we'll make it ladies night. Cherry could use the night out, too, I'm sure."

I smiled. It was so kind of her to offer, or to include me with her group of friends, but with all my secrets and shame, I wasn't really into forming close friendships. I didn't want Sky to hate me, either, though. "Well..."

"Come on. You've already met everyone. And before you think that things might be awkward what with the Armand thing and how that turned out, let me assure you there's nothing to worry about. The guys won't be anywhere in sight—no guys allowed. "

I wrinkled my nose in confusion. "What do you mean the Armand thing?"

She was partly distracted with keeping Mia from ripping her earing out. "He mentioned that he was ending things between the two of you. I'm sorry that I know. That kind of stuff is so uncomfortable, and I'd hate for you to feel awkward around us. He's got, shall we say, a life plan. One day, he'll settle down, but until then, I think you dodged a painful bullet."

"Oh. He mentioned..." I just blinked at her for a few seconds. "When did he mention that?"

Her cheeks went bright red. "A couple of days ago... Angel, did he not say anything?"

My heart sank into my stomach like a lead balloon. Armand talked to Sky about ending things with me? What else was Armand saying about me behind my back? I wanted desperately to laugh as though I was unaffected—to wave my hand in the air dismissively like I couldn't care less what Armand did or didn't do. But the truth was, I felt utterly sick. "H-he must've forgotten."

She squeezed her eyes shut. "Oh, lordy, I am so, so sorry. I should not have opened my big mouth."

I managed a smile, although it was more like a grimace. "It's fine. We're not serious. I just wish he would've just said something." I dug my fingernails into my palm.

I was an idiot. I wondered if he laughed at what an easy booty call I was. Why did he want to end things? Was I too much reality, with a baby and all? Armand seemed to love Mia. He certainly brought enough gifts for her—for both of us. I couldn't imagine it was all just to get in my pants. Armand was a good-looking man—very good looking—alright, he was drop-dead gorgeous. Way too hot to stick around with someone like me for any length of time. Had he met an equally hot woman? Maybe that was it. He met someone else and didn't have the balls to end things with me to my face.

"You have to let me take you out now. I mean, come on. After my loose lips? I'll buy all of your drinks and whatever drunken snacks you could possibly want. Anything."

I started to shake my head, but when tears threatened, I reconsidered. Sure, I wanted to go home, curl up in a ball and cry, but what if Armand showed up later? He told Sky he was ending things a few days ago, but he held me in his arms just last night. How humiliating.

If he did show up, and chances were pretty good he would, I wanted to stand tall and tell him to get his booty-calling ass far away from me and never come back. I was not prepared for that kind of confrontation yet, though.

Then again, what if he didn't show at all? What if he just ghosted me? Then I would be alone wallowing in my humiliation. Screw that. I would make sure I was unavailable tonight when Armand showed up to slip into my bed. I'd ghost him. Ha!

"You know what? Sure."

She grinned. "Good! We can leave the kids with Beast and Cezar. They'll take good care of them."

I shook my head. "I have a nanny on-call when I need her. She'll be thrilled for the chance to sit with Mia."

"I really am sorry, Angel. I didn't mean to open my big mouth and let—"

"You're not at fault. You assumed that he'd done what he said he was going to do. You couldn't have known that he's been in my bed every night for almost a month." I frowned. I hated that I said that out loud. It seemed that in my frustration, anger and shame, my mouth was working faster than my mind. "I'm just... I'm angry and I'm angry that I'm angry. I don't even have a right to be angry. I mean, I made the rules and I was very adamant about them. I made sure to spell out that we were just hooking up. Nothing more."

She nodded. "I can have Beast tell him that we're going out tonight so he can't warm your bed for you."

I shrugged. "No, he'll figure it out when he shows up and I'm not there." Two can play the brush-off game.

She laughed. "Good point. Okay, tonight then. We can pick you up."

I shook my head. "I'll take an Uber. Just tell me when and where."

She pulled out her phone and handed it to me. "Put your number in and I'll call you with the details."

I did just that and then took Mia from her. "I'm going to head back out and try to find something to wear tonight."

"Something sexy."

I smiled feebly. "Sounds like a plan."

"I still feel like a giant loose-lipped turd. Can I give you a free slice of pie?"

Trying to sound casual, I forced a laugh, which ended up sounded just like a forced laugh, and shook my head. "I'm fine, Sky. Thanks, though. I'll see you tonight."

Sky still wore a slightly worried expression as she watched me leave with Mia. With every minute that passed, my initial shock and anger and outrage turned to sorrow and depression.

This whole thing was my own fault. I'm the idiot who fell for Armand. He was just supposed to be a casual hookup, but my stupid heart latched onto him. Now that he wanted to end our trysts, I was devastated? I deserved to be devastated, to have to watch him walk away like I was nothing to him. I *was* nothing to him. I was always nothing. Except to Mia. I looked down at the little sleeping princess in my arms. To Mia, I was everything.

Chapter Eighteen

ANGEL

Even though my hands shook as I left Mia with her nanny, I forced myself to hand her over. I reminded myself that Mrs. Schumacher, an older woman with greying temples, had tons of childcare experience and had been carefully vetted through the agency.

Part of me was afraid that Armand would show up before I could leave and I'd have to have a confrontation with him before I was ready. Another part of me hoped he would show up, tearfully express what a mistake he'd made in choosing to leave me, and drop to his knees begging for another chance—yeah, right.

I had calmed somewhat since Sky dropped the bomb on me earlier. I knew that as difficult as it was for me to swallow, it was for the best. It was better for Armand to get away from me. No matter what I wanted, he needed to go.

I caught an Uber to take me to the address Sky had texted me, a bar called the Catfish Brewery. I was uncharacteristically upbeat about spending the evening out. I had an excuse to drink until I was numb. I was looking forward to a respite from the conflicting emotions rampaging through my brain. The choice I needed to make about Mia and the loss of Armand were resting heavily on my shoulders. Tonight would be a temporary reprieve from all the weighty issues dragging me down—make everything go away for a couple of hours.

I was wearing a killer dress. I'd dug back in my closet for just the right thing to turn heads and boost my self-esteem. It was a little tight, since I still had a few leftover pounds on me from pregnancy, but the snug fit enhanced my figure rather than detract from it. I even went a little easier on the goth look—ditched the dark eye makeup and swapped the black lipstick for red.

As the Uber pulled up in front of Catfish Brewery, I started to reconsider this ladies' night. Did I think I would be able to flirt with other men? Dance, laugh, have a good time? Not with the sick, burning, sinking feeling in my middle that would not go away. As much as I wanted to forget it and brush it off, the situation with Armand was incredibly painful and I felt myself self-destructing. I could feel my seams easing apart until the only thing holding me together was the tight dress I'd squeezed into.

Still, I got out of the Uber and forced a smile when I spotted Sky and Cherry standing there on the sidewalk out front. I stood straight and pretended that I wasn't having an emotional crisis.

"Wow!" Sky reached out and took my hand. "You look stunning."

Cherry nodded. "Girl, how the hell did you lose your baby weight so fast?"

I laughed and winced when it sounded shaky. "It's still here. It's just squeezed into shapewear."

"I need that brand." Cherry nodded in the direction of the entrance. "Ready? Chyna and Lennox are on their way. They'll meet us late tonight."

"Late tonight?"

Sky waved off my question. "Cherry's a librarian. Anything after 8:30 is late to her."

Cherry smiled politely at the bouncer who opened the door for us. "We're out for the first time in forever. The guys hardly ever back off enough for us to have fun without them. We're partying it up tonight." She turned to Sky, whispering. "In truth, I wouldn't be surprised if they take turns perched on the roof keeping watch over us."

Sky snorted and the two of them looked at one another as though sharing a private joke. I was about to ask what that meant when Cherry suddenly stopped moving in front of me and I bumped into her back. I started to apologize, but she whipped around to me, eyes like saucers, and shook her head. "This place is a dud. Let's go somewhere else."

"What? Cherry—" Sky started to protest, then stopped and abruptly turned to me, nodding. "Yeah, uh, this place is dead tonight. Let's get out of here."

My eyes shifted over Cherry's shoulder, a magnetic draw pulling them in that direction. The same magnetism that had gotten me in the mess I was in to begin with.

Sitting at the bar with a sleazy-looking woman draped over him was Armand. He looked bored, but the woman who suddenly turned and planted herself on his lap didn't seem to notice or care as she rocked her hips against him. As I watched, she turned and snaked her arms around the back of Armand's muscled neck.

The blood in my veins turned to concrete. Other people were moving around me, trying to get into the bar, but I was frozen. I'd never actually seen one of my boyfriends cheat before. I knew Alan Dougerson had had a side chick, but I'd never seen them together with my own eyes.

Ugh, what was I thinking? Armand was not my boyfriend! And that had been my choice. He couldn't exactly be cheating on me if he wasn't my boyfriend, could he?

The next few seconds seemed to pass in slow motion. I didn't know what I was expecting. Armand to jump up and drop her on her ass for daring to come on to him when he didn't want it? Or, did he want it?

"Oh, Angel, let's go." Sky took my hand and tugged me back a step.

"Angel. Come on, honey." Cherry cupped the back of my arm and tried to ease me away.

As quiet and frozen-still as I was, it seemed like it was enough to draw attention to me—including Armand's. His eyes snapped to mine and he had the decency to pale. The woman nearly fell to the floor when he stood up suddenly.

I shook my head because the last thing I wanted was for him to come over to me and have everyone see me lose my shit all over the place.

Finally, with Sky and Cherry's prodding, I was able to get my feet to work, and I walked out on rubbery legs.

Back out on the sidewalk, as the first tear escaped, it became abundantly clear that the dress wasn't going to be enough to hold me together after all.

Sky somehow conjured up an Uber out of thin air and the three of us piled into the back, heading away from the Catfish Brewery.

Even though I knew Armand and I were just friends with benefits and we hadn't even discussed exclusivity, I still felt betrayed. That was on me, though.

Tears fell as my chest throbbed. Seeing him with someone else had the kick-in-the-head effect of showing me just how much I liked him and wanted him. The pain was shocking. I couldn't remember the loss of any other man hurting that way. I begged anger to come back, but it was nowhere to be found. The only emotion at the forefront, as the women forced my address out of me and got the driver to take us to my house, was unending sorrow and a deep sense of loss.

"I'm so sorry, Angel. I wish that hadn't happened." Sky stroked my hair and kept it out of my face. "I'm going to kill him."

Cherry snorted. "Not if I kill him first."

They kept their questions to themselves as I opened the wrought iron gate to the property using the remote I dug out of my purse. The Uber transported us past the wall of the estate, onto the vast grounds, and toward the mansion proper. I could see the curiosity when I glanced at the women on either side of me, but none said a word. Lips pressed tightly, they just followed me up the stairs, across the wide wraparound porch, and through the front door into the receiving foyer. Inside the house, the three of us tromped up the grand staircase and through the vast hallway lined with antique benches, old portraits, oil paintings of landscapes, and family memorabilia. As we entered Mia's nursery, Mrs. Schumacher was shocked to see me back so soon, but she didn't ask questions, either. She pressed a kiss to Mia's head before handing her off to me to leave.

"Oh, Angel, she's beautiful." Cherry ran a finger over Mia's hair and smiled. "And look at all that hair!"

I laughed through my tears, something about holding Mia released some of the pain. At least I still had her—for the time being anyway. As I held her tight to my chest, I plopped down in the rocker next to her crib, suddenly exhausted.

"Do you want us to stay with you or do you want to be alone?" Sky was already sitting on the floor across from me, though. And before I could formulate an answer, she added, "Like we'd leave you when you're this upset. I just asked to be polite."

Cherry sat next to her and sighed. "Men are so stupid."

I shook my head and stared up at the ceiling. "I'm so stupid."

"What? No. This isn't on you."

"I should've known better. It was selfish of me to get involved with him anyway, knowing what could've happened." I looked down at Mia. "So selfish."

Cherry sat forward. "What are you talking about?"

"I know you know. Sky must have told you. The Angel of Death stuff."

"Angel of Death stuff?"

Everyone around me dies. I'm a curse, a hex on anyone around me."

Cherry laughed but quieted when she realized I wasn't joking. "Oh, my god. You're serious. You really believe that?"

"It's the truth. I can't even handle it anymore. I can't watch another person die knowing I'm responsible." My finger gently stroked Mia's baby soft curls. "And don't try to tell me I'm not Angel of Death, that it's all superstitious mumbo jumbo, because I won't believe you."

I buried my nose in the blanket Mia was swaddled in, breathing in the sweet baby smell. When I looked up, both Sky and Cherry were staring at me, with open mouths and wide eyes. I blew out a slow breath. I supposed I would have to explain.

"My parents died in a fiery plane crash, my grandmother was killed in a terrible fall down the stairs, and my uncle met his end in a freak accident. Every boyfriend I've ever had is now pushing up daisies... I'm glad Armand got away. Truly."

As I spoke the words, my tears returned with a vengeance. My heart was broken—shattered—but I truly believed that it was the for the best. "I would not have survived having to watch Armand die, too. I would not have survived it. And, mark my words, if he stayed with me, he'd have died. They all do. And I never would have recovered. Not ever."

There were several minutes of stunned silence. Then Sky started to shake her head. I knew she was about to protest, but she hadn't heard everything yet.

I leveled her with a stare. "If anyone should believe me, it's you."

"What? Why me?"

I kissed Mia's head again and sobbed. "Amie and Jeremiah. I carried Mia for them. I was their surrogate. Look how that ended."

Sky's hand went over her heart, and her eyes filled with emotion, but she shook her head. "Angel, you didn't do that."

"Yes, yes, I did. As sure as if I'd been driving the car that sent them careening over the median and into oncoming traffic. I killed Amie and Jeremiah."

Chapter Nineteen

ARMAND

I went straight to Angel's house.

What had I been thinking, listening to Beast? I'd gone out and halfheartedly continued to look for a mate simply because of the promise I'd made to him. A ridiculous promise. A promise that never should have passed over my lips.

I knew Angel wouldn't want to see me, and I didn't blame her, but I needed to explain. I would plead with her to allow me to explain. I would tell her the truth—all of it. I would tell her of my dragon, the coming eclipse, the fact that I despised being near any other female and thought only of her night and day.

I would convince her that she was the only female I wanted from now until the end of my days. I would, without question or remorse, sacrifice eternal life for the chance to spend the next few months, days, hours, or minutes—however much time I had left—with her.

When I arrived, I found Angel's gate locked, but that didn't stop me. I climbed over and let myself in. I took the stairs two at a time and heard her crying in Mia's room. I was about to rush in when I heard Cherry's voice.

"What are you talking about?"

Angel's reply came out with a sob. "I know you know. The Angel of Death stuff."

"Angel of Death stuff?"

"Everyone around me dies. I'm a curse, a hex, on anyone around me."

I did not know what Angel was talking about. What would make her think such a thing?

Cherry laughed, but then her voice turned serious. "Oh, my god. You're serious. You really believe that?"

"It's the truth. I can't even handle it anymore. I can't watch another person die knowing I'm responsible. And don't try to tell me I'm not Angel of Death, that it's all superstitious mumbo jumbo, because I won't believe you. My parents died in a fiery plane crash, my grandmother was killed in a terrible fall down the stairs, and my uncle meet his end in a freak accident. Every boyfriend I've ever had is now pushing up daisies... I'm glad Armand got away. Truly. I would not have survived having to watch Armand die, too. I would not have survived it. And, mark my words, if he stayed with me, he'd have died. They all do. And I never would have recovered. Not ever."

As her words sank in, I slowly backed away from the door, supporting myself against the wall. I had no idea of this burden Angel carried. Here I was, seconds away from asking her—begging her—to allow me to remain with her and Mia, and then in a few months' time, watch me die.

I was truly a selfish dragon.

I had to physically restrain the beast inside from surging forward. He didn't want to leave her. He could smell and taste her tears, and he wanted to go to her. But I knew Angel and I were not to be.

I could not ask Angel to watch me die so that I might spend my remaining days with her. I had caused her enough pain; the kindest thing I could do now was to leave her alone.

I quietly crept away, down the stairs and then outside, where I shifted, my clothes shredding away. I flew over the landscape, over the marshes and swamps and small towns, and out over the ocean in an attempt to soothe my breaking heart.

I considered opening a link to Ovide and sharing my problems with him, but I thought better of it. Ovide had plenty of his own darkness without borrowing mine.

After several hours of flying aimlessly over the ocean waves, I returned home.

As I stood under a steaming hot shower, letting the water cascade over my head and shoulders, I gave in to feeling sorry for myself. I wanted desperately for Angel to be my mate. Things were so easy with her. Being with her was as natural as breathing, and my longing for her, my attraction, was unlike anything I had ever experienced.

For her own good, I had to give her up before she blamed herself for my destined demise. My soul ached at the loss. I could never return to her house, never again hold her as she slept. I could never watch little Mia grow—take her first steps, speak her first word, go to school, learn to read and write. I hung my head and sagged against the tile wall as my tears mixed with the spray from the shower.

I exited the shower long after the water turned cold. Pain radiated out from my chest. I'd never hated being a dragon before, even through the bad times when we were being hunted and had to run for our lives. I never once wished I was anything other than the way I'd been born. But at that moment, however, I cursed my race. I wanted the freedom to love freely. I wanted to be with Angel and Mia.

I didn't understand this agony I was suffering. I'd never heard of a female who was not his mate causing a dragon so much pain. Yet, everything in me told me Angel was mine.

What if we were all wrong? We assumed that females who were fated to become our mates were compelled to remain virgins until mated. It was something that was always true in the old world. Their interest in sex was sparked only by their mates, which was why a dragon male was obliged to always put his mate's pleasure first. It was a dragon's honor to place his female's needs above his own. But what if the rules of nature were different here in the new world? What if things were different with mates who were human?

Although, my brethren on this planet had all so far mated females who were virgins, so I supposed I was just grasping at straws.

I slumped onto my bed and sent out a link to Beast.

Did you ever have feelings for a woman before Sky?

Impossible. A dragon only falls for his mate. You know that. So, whatever has happened between you and Angel is not real. Whatever you are feeling is not true. You are simply desperate to find your mate before the eclipse.

Anger scorched through me so quickly and so fiercely that a burst of flames shot forth from my lips and lit my bedding on fire. I swore at Beast as I put it out.

Do not tell me how I feel! I know how I feel! Desperation has nothing to do with what I feel for Angel. Nothing!

Beast sighed. *I apologize. I just think you want it too much. She is not your mate. She has a youngling. You know how it works, brother.*

I closed the connection with him and walked outside naked to get a few flasks from my collection. I would not sleep this night, of that I was certain.

Settling at the end of my dock with my feet in the water, I opened the first bottle and took a long drag. I no longer had a will to survive. And, I certainly had no will to find a mate.

The search for a mate was over for me. My time was nearing its end, and I was okay with that. Whether they liked it or not, when the time came, when I finally lost control of my faculties, my fellow dragons would end me.

But before that day, I would beg one last favor from them. I could not leave this life without knowing Angel and Mia were safe. From each one of my brethren, I would exact a solemn vow: Look after my girls after I was gone.

Chapter Twenty

ANGEL

"I didn't want to believe at first that I was Angel of Death, either."

Lennox and Chyna had come straight here after Sky had discretely slipped away and called them. The five of us were curled up, each on one end of the three overstuffed antique sofas in the study. Cherry had gathered pillows and blankets from all over the house, and Sky had moved the sofas so they surrounded the fireplace hearth.

"Stupid me was so tired of being laughed at, pointed to, and ridiculed. I was tired of being the bringer of death, so late one night, I had this brilliant idea: I'd bring forth life." I fidgeted with the baby monitor on my lap as the four women listened quietly. "I Googled surrogacy agencies, and before I even gave any serious thought to what I was doing, I filled out the application."

"Part of the application process included a medical examination, and that's where I met Amie, at Dr. Alvin Brown's office. Unfortunately, someone in the reception area recognized me, started shouting that I was the bringer of all things unholy, and well, the ranting cleared out the office."

Chyna tsk-ed behind her teeth, and Lennox shook her head, seemingly horrified. "That's awful!"

"Amie was awesome, though. She called them superstitious crazies and woo-woo junkies." I smiled at the memory. Then my smile turned to a frown. I would have begun sobbing again, but it seemed all my tears had been used up for the night. I was bordering on numbness.

"We got to talking, and it turned out that Amie and Jeremiah had all but given up on having kids. They were saving for a surrogate and an egg donor, since not only was Amie not capable of carrying a child, her eggs weren't viable, either. But the combined paychecks of a waitress and a carpenter didn't stretch far. You don't even know how excited I was to hear Amie's story. I know it sounds terrible that I was relishing in another's sorrow, but I saw it as my chance to help—to give a new little life to a couple who desperately wanted one. It was to be my redemption. Or, so I thought."

As my eyes grew droopy from fatigue, the exhaustion of a hard cry, and the wafting smoke from the fireplace, I yawned, starting a chain reaction.

"We didn't go through an agency. I paid for the egg donor, and the in vitro."

Cherry sat up. "You *paid* for it, too?"

I nodded. "Well, Amie swore it was a loan and that she and Jeremiah would pay me back every penny, but I didn't care if she did or didn't. I desperately wanted not to be Angel of Death anymore." I watched the flames dance in the fireplace as the memories played in front of my eyes. Yeah, what I had hoped would be my redemption turned out to be the death of two wonderful people whose only fault was they wanted desperately to be parents."

That thought was the last thing I remembered until I was startled awake by Mia's hungry cries transmitted through the baby monitor.

———

Somehow, my home had been invaded. After our impromptu slumber-slash-pity party the night before, the significant others of the four women who'd stayed with me showed up. They brought groceries and, of course, Cezar brought his and Cherry's daughter, Molly. They seemed reluctant to leave me alone.

The men were talking and laughing, and the women were smiling. Everyone was happy—glowing, even. Everyone but me.

I was the polar opposite of glowing. My skin was dull, and I had a stress breakout on my chin. My eyes were red and swollen; my hair was dirty. I had stripped my shapewear off, but I was somehow still wearing the dress from the night before, with a pair of pajama pants added under it. I felt...drained.

All I wanted to do was hold Mia in my arms forever, but I had come to a decision. It was time. My secret was out. Mia wasn't mine. A part of me had almost expected Sky to snatch her from my arms like the zombies in my nightmares. That didn't happen, though.

Despite my offer of having an on-call chef come in, Sky insisted on cooking breakfast for us. If they noticed that I was silent as they talked among themselves, they didn't say anything. They let me be.

I'd certainly felt the pain of loss before, but I couldn't remember ever feeling it so deeply. I had come to a decision, and the time to implement it was now.

I stood up, eyes locked on little Mia in my arms. She meant everything to me, my little princess. I wanted to wrap her up and keep her forever, but it wasn't about what I wanted.

"Will you be the one to take Mia to Amie's family?" My question was directed at Sky, but my teary eyes remained on Mia.

The kitchen fell silent. Sky quietly put down the spatula she'd been holding and turned to face me. "Um...I suppose I could do that. But you should come with me, if that's truly what you want. I don't know if it's the best plan of action, though. Amie's parents aren't exactly...familial."

Pain radiated through me. "Jeremiah has no family."

"Angel...what are you talking about?"

"I wasn't supposed to keep her. She was supposed to be Amie and Jeremiah's baby. By keeping her, I'm in essence kidnapping her. She isn't mine, and I'm pretending like she is." Suddenly, Mia started screaming in my arms, her little face red, scrunched up, and her toothless mouth wide open. "I'm sorry, my little princess. I'm so sorry."

Sky rushed around the kitchen to me. "Angel, are you sure this is what you want?"

Of course, it wasn't. I loved Mia more than I loved myself, which was exactly why I was doing this. I was so choked up, I couldn't speak to respond to Sky's question. Lips pressed tightly together to contain the wrenching sobs trying to escape, and I merely nodded.

I tried to hand Mia to Sky, but she shook her head.

"Wait. Think this through. You're where she belongs. I know you really believe all this Angel of Death mumbo jumbo, but it's not true."

"It's easy to say that it's not true when there isn't a pile of bodies in your wake." My voice came out sharper than I meant it to, but I was also trying to speak over Mia's wailing. "Every single person around me dies."

"What about us? We've all been around you. We're fine."

"So far." I sank back into my chair and rocked Mia, trying to soothe her. "She deserves better."

Sky growled and shook her head. "This is crazy. I'm not letting you give up that baby because of some bullpucky about a death curse. People die. Everyone dies. Sure, you've had to endure the deaths of more friends and family than some people, but that does not mean that you're to blame for any of it. Some dipwad just cooked that story up to sell newspapers and make a name for himself. I know that you'd planned to give Mia to Amie and Jeremiah, but life throws us curve balls sometimes, and now she's yours. If you want to give her up, that's one thing, but don't do it because of some superstitious rubbish. You'd hate yourself forever, Angel. I see how much you love her."

"I don't *want* to give her up." I was full out sobbing, competing with Mia over who could cry the loudest. "I *have* to give her up."

"Fine." Sky grabbed Mia from my arms and shrugged. "Amie's parents live in New Orleans. I can look them up and have her with them in a few hours' time."

Sky didn't get more than three steps away when I leaped up and grabbed her arm to stop her. It didn't deter her, though. She just pulled away from me and kept walking toward the door.

My heart slammed against my rib cage and something raged from inside me. The idea of someone taking my baby brought fury burning through me, and I opened my mouth and let out a scream that seemed to rattle the house. Somewhere it turned into a growl and all I could do was stand there and shake as it consumed me.

Sky turned to me and her mouth hung open. Mia's screams instantly stopped. "What the holy H-E-double-toothpicks was that?"

I held my hands out for Mia and growled. "She. Stays. With. Me."

"What *was* that?" Cherry came running over with Molly cradled in her arms, her eyes just as wide as Sky's.

Sky's head was tilted as she studied me. Wearing a huge grin, she placed Mia in my arms. "Now, that's more like it, Mama."

I pulled Mia into my chest and felt instantly calmer. It had been like I was floating over my body in a rage, but with Mia, I came back down and settled. "Sorry. I just...I can't let her go. I know I should, but I can't."

"Honey, you just became a mama bear protecting her cub." Lennox grinned at me as she came over. "It was awesome."

"More like a mama dragon." Sky reached out and cupped my cheek. "Oh, sweetie. You are her mommy."

Suddenly, she made a face. Her hand fell from my cheek and covered her mouth. "I hate to keep dragging all your personal secrets out, but this one's important. When you and Armand first slept together, you weren't by any chance...a virgin...*were you?*"

"What?" My cheeks heated, and I rocked Mia to try to calm myself. What kind of a question was that?

"Oh, my god!" Cherry swung around and stared at me like the right answer to the question might win me a million dollars.

Chyna scrunched up her nose as her hand absently rested on her now enormous baby bump. "It sounds so awful, that question, but trust us, it's important."

Lennox dropped down in front of the rocker and rested her hands on my knees. "We all assumed, because of the baby...but you were a virgin, weren't you, Angel?"

My face was bright red. What the hell had come over the four of them? With an embarrassed nod, I looked away. "Yeah, I was."

Lennox suddenly squealed and grabbed me. "This makes so much more sense."

Sky leaned in abruptly and planted a kiss on Mia's head and then my cheek. "We have so much to talk about, Angel. Don't worry, though, everything will work out fine."

Then, almost in unison, they all said, "Welcome to the family."

Chapter Twenty-One

ANGEL

I wasn't sure what they were all of a sudden so giddy and giggly about.

Finally, it was Beast who began the explanation. "We assumed that you were not Armand's mate. Since you were with young, we thought..." he cleared his throat, "I thought..."

Sky nudged him out of the way and popped her head in my line of vision. "No, we all thought it. Now, we're all pretty doggone sure that you are Armand's mate."

I scowled. "If I was Armand's soulmate, do you think he'd be out at bars letting random women hang all over him? I don't."

Sky blew out a deep breath. "That might've been partially my fault."

"Or mine." Beast looked uncharacteristically sheepish.

I narrowed my eyes and almost asked what they meant, but then thought better about it. "No matter what you two think you did, neither of you forced Armand to do anything he didn't want to do. That was his choice. And if I was his soulmate, he'd have made a different choice. It's fine, guys. It's all good. I was a booty call. A slut. You don't have to try to sugarcoat it."

Cezar covered Molly's ears and growled. "Do not speak about your-self like that."

Cherry held her hand over her heart as she looked at her man. "Cezar's right. No slut-shaming. As a single woman, you can sleep with whomever you want. You weren't a booty call. He was."

"Uh, Cherry, not helping." Chyna gave her a pointed look. "Look, even when Sky was scolding Armand to stay away from you, he couldn't stop. He has feelings for you, he does."

My brain hurt. I wanted to go upstairs and curl up for a nap. "I-I can't make sense of anything that's happening right now. You all did a 180 on the Armand situation. But it doesn't really matter who warned whom away from whom. It's over. He's gone and I'm fine... I will be...someday."

Sky looked at Beast and seemed to silently give him an order. When she looked back at me, she frowned. "We've been keeping something from you."

Beast stood up and nodded to the backyard. "Please follow us."

For some reason, I did. I followed the group of lunatics into my backyard. I had no idea what tricks they had up their sleeves, but when Beast started stripping, I held up my hands and waved them in front of me. "Nope, no. If y'all are about to tell me you're some free-lovin' swinger orgy group, save it. I'm not into that lifestyle, and I'm not condoning any such goings-on in my backyard."

Sky giggled. "No worries. It's nothing even remotely like that. Go on, look."

By the time I turned my head in the direction she was pointing, toward where Beast had stood, he was gone. In his place was a huge, black and gold scaly monster...a...a dragon? I scrunched my eyebrows and dug my fists into my hips as though I might scowl it away. But...no, there was still a giant dragon in my yard. "D-did that thing eat Beast?"

A chorus of roaring laughter arose and then faded along with the rest of the world as the blue cloudy sky suddenly became all I could see. Then blackness.

When I came back around, I was lying on the sofa in the formal drawing room. Beast stood over me, and I was relieved for Sky. The dragon hadn't eaten her mate. *Dragon?* It all came crashing back, and I sat straight up.

"Whoa, you're okay. Just stay where you are, Angel." Beast held his hands out, and I noticed his arms were bare. So was his chest. When he noticed me looking, he actually crossed his arms over his chest and cleared his throat. "I had no time to put on my shirt."

Sky appeared next to me and draped a damp cloth over my forehead. "You scared us."

"*I* scared *you*?" I took the cloth off and attempted to stand. Shaky at first, I quickly gained my footing and walked to the other side of the room. "What the fuck was that? I thought something had killed you, Beast. I thought that my curse nabbed you. I thought a giant reptilian overlord landed in my yard and ate you! Dear god, what am I saying? My curse has used car crashes, plane crashes, falls, deadly diseases, poisonous snakes, but that would've been the wildest one ever. Death by a giant dragon."

They all just stared at me.

"Dragon..." I stopped rambling and ran my hands through my hair. "Did I really just see a dragon?"

Sky nodded. "Yeah."

"How?"

Beast raised his hand. "That would be me."

"You have a pet dragon?" I screamed the question and then shook my head. "Sorry, I don't mean to scream at you. It's just not every day I see a pet dragon."

"I do not have a pet dragon."

Sky giggled. "He's *my* pet dragon."

Beast growled and waggled his eyebrows.

I just stood there, gaping. Everyone was standing around my living room staring at me, and it was the most awkward thing that I could've ever imagined. I felt like I was on the outside of an inside joke they all shared. Everyone was waiting for me to catch on, but I was too stupid to get it.

"I *am* a dragon, Angel." Beast waved to the other men. "We are all dragons."

Blaise nodded. "As is Armand."

I snorted. "Armand is a dragon? Armand? Really, guys?" I shook my head. "This is ridiculous."

Sky held up her hands and frowned. "Maybe this wasn't the best way to reveal it to you, but I didn't know how else to do it. I had a hard time accepting it at first myself."

"Me, too. It's wild, isn't it?" Cherry shrugged. "It's real, though."

Lennox, who was holding Mia and making goo-goo faces at her, nodded. "I found out by watching Remy's drunk dragon fall from the sky and then turn into a very naked man."

"Prove it." I stalked over to the door to the yard and swung it open. Go out there and turn into a dragon. Fly a lap around the grounds, if you'd like."

Beast snarled at me. "You have quite an attitude. I see why you and Armand are fated mates."

"Do not say his name right now."

Sky laughed and slapped her mate on the butt. "You heard her. Fly, big guy."

With a lot of growling and grunting, Beast walked out into the yard and stripped down before shifting into, yep, a giant dragon. Then, he lifted off into the air and flew a lap around my yard. When he landed and shifted back into his human self, he did it with a scowl in my direction.

I just nodded. "And here I thought you guys were mercenaries."

"We have more to talk about. More about Armand." Sky gently touched my arm, like she was worried about startling me.

"Not right now. I need time to process what I just saw." I took Mia from Lennox's arms. "Thank you all for coming; it's been real. I need to be alone now."

"One more thing?" Sky said hopefully. "It was my fault that Armand did what he did. I told him to stay away from you. I had no idea you were mates. I thought he'd hurt you. He never wanted to, though. He's a good guy, really."

I nodded to the door. "I don't want to talk about him."

Cherry wrapped her arms around me and was instantly joined by Chyna and Lenni. Their warmth melted a little of the shock away some and when I looked back at them, I couldn't help a tiny smile.

"Just go."

"You'll call?" Sky caught my hand and gave me her best puppy dog eyes. "Please?"

"Sure. Now, g'won, all of you. And don't forget your dragons."

Chapter Twenty-Two

ARMAND

You must get over to my castle immediately. I have a wonderful surprise for you. Beast's thoughts projected into my psyche were not a welcome intrusion.

My head throbbed painfully. I'd been on a bender, drinking nearly everything in my stash—all to try to forget *her*. Just moving made my stomach lurch. *Go away.*

Cezar's voice was next. *Get over here now, brother, this is important.*

Cherry never missed a chance to yell into our heads. *Stop feeling sorry for yourself, Armand. It's good news, and it's about Angel. You can thank us later.*

I sat up and gagged. My teeth felt like they were wearing fuzzy little sweaters. *Angel?*

I growled and tried to stumble to my feet. I didn't realize I had fallen asleep on my dock and, and as I rolled over, I fell off and splashed into the ocean. The ice-cold water was a shock to my system, but it did nothing to quell the roiling in my stomach. I hadn't the energy to swim back to shore or even climb out of the water, so I let my dragon burst free for the first time in days.

I had been fighting my dragon for three days. For three days, I had managed to stay away from Angel, and every second had been torturous. I had to fight with my dragon constantly to keep from shifting and making a beeline for her. For three days, I moped, wallowed, and drank myself stupid.

I did not know what it was about Angel the others wanted to discuss, but I was starved for any news about her. As I neared Beast's swamp, a strange tingling came over me. The closer I got, the more it grew. It was almost as if... And there she was!

I gasped in shock to see Angel standing in the middle of Beast's patio with Mia in her arms, pointing at Remy, Blaise, Cezar, Beast, and...even Ovide was there. They were all in their dragon forms, flying overhead, ducking and dodging one another, nosediving into the swamp and shooting straight back into the sky.

I had no idea what was going on. It was as if I'd stepped into a dreamscape while wide awake. My dragon landed as close to Angel as he could and practically rolled over onto his belly for her.

I watched as her jaw dropped, tears filled her eyes, and then anger emerged. She turned away and marched into the house, leaving me with a gaping hole in my heart and the urge to crawl into the lake and drown myself.

When I forced my dragon to retreat and shifted back, he was too weakened by sorrow to fight it.

I looked around at the other dragons. "What is this? Why is Angel here, and why does she know—"

Beast opened his mouth to speak, but a commotion near the house drew our attention. Angel was marching out, arguing with Sky.

"How dare you! I didn't ask for that. You should've known better after the last time you interfered."

Sky hurried behind Angel, looking contrite. "You know why I had them call him over. We explained everything to you."

"And I explained everything to you. It doesn't appear that you heard me, though. I'm ready to leave, now." Angel swung her head in my direction and froze as our eyes met. Then her eyes clouded over and looked away as she adjusted Mia. "Is there a boat anywhere I can borrow? Or is the only transportation around here today dragon back?"

Sky groaned. "You're stubborn."

"And you're meddling."

Beast sighed. "Your female is always ready to fight."

I stared at Angel, willing her with all my might to look at me. "I know how nature has traditionally presented mates, but maybe the rules don't always apply. Maybe this is a special mating. We all know it isn't supposed to happen this way, but I feel as if she is mine. And if she is not, then I do not want a mate."

Beast slapped my back and laughed. "Or the natural tradition is present and we were technologically behind enough not to realize it. It is possible now to become impregnated while a virgin."

"Beast, can you fire up the mud boat and give Angel a ride home?"

I growled before I even knew what I was doing.

"Did you hear what I said, Armand?"

Angel turned to us. "Come on, just let me use your boat."

"I will take you home." I declared, leaving her no room to argue. She was my female, no matter what the laws of nature declared. My dragon knew it and I knew it.

She spun and pointed her finger angrily in my direction. "You are not taking me anywhere!"

Beast slapped me on the back. "I said she was a virgin when she got pregnant. A *virgin*."

I snapped my head around to him. "What?"

"Oh, my god!" Angel screamed from across the yard, upsetting Mia. "You took my virginity. Does anyone else want to talk about my sex life? Are there no topics that are off limits with you people? If I can't get a ride home in two seconds with someone who is not Armand, I'm going to start swimming!"

Ovide's dragon appeared, and he chuffed at Angel before motioning his head toward his back. I couldn't do anything more than watch as she climbed onto his back with Mia strapped to her chest in one of the sling carriers I had gifted them. I watched helplessly as Ovide took to the sky.

I hated that she had accepted a ride from another male. Although, I was somewhat comforted by the fact that the male was Ovide. Ovide didn't even like women. Not that he was gay. He wasn't. He didn't like men, either. Ovide didn't like anyone.

I turned and glared at Beast. "I am going to flame you to ashes if you knew. You told me she was not my mate and forced a promise from my lips to continue to look for another female!"

Beast, to his credit, appeared to look remorseful as he shrugged. Then he opened his big scaly mouth. "You allowed your mate to fly off with Ovide."

I glowered at Beast. "I do not understand this!" I turned to the other dragons. "Can someone explain it to me?"

Blaise was shaking his head as though he, too, was baffled. "Apparently, humans have this thing where if a female is unable to grow a child in her belly, another female will do it for her."

Remy added, "Yet, the male does not mount her."

I scratched the back of my neck. "Does not mount her? How is that so?"

Cezar spread his hands to the side and shrugged. "According to Cherry, it is done in a medical facility using surgical tools."

"Oh, for heaven's sake." Sky took my arm and led me toward the house. "The fertilized egg is implanted into a woman who will act as a surrogate and carry and birth the baby for the other couple. That's what Angel did. She was a surrogate for the woman I worked with, Amie, and her husband, Jeremiah. Only, before Mia was born, they were killed in an automobile accident."

"You knew this? You told me to stay away from Angel, yet you knew this?"

"No! Of course not, Armand. None of us did. I'm really sorry."

I was pathetic. All I wanted to do was find Angel and tell her how sorry I was. She was my mate, and she saw another female touching me. The pain I must've caused her... Just the thought was a knife to the gut.

I had no choice but to go to Angel and beg her forgiveness. Then, if she would allow, I would spend eternity making up to her.

Chapter Twenty-Three
ANGEL

"Thank you, Ovide. I owe you." I had my head turned away as I handed him my oversized pink chenille bathrobe. It was the only piece of clothing I owned that was big enough to fit him.

"You owe me nothing."

I turned back to him and smiled the best smile I could muster at that moment. Seeing Armand had hurt. He'd looked so rough. I could almost imagine that he'd been pining away for me, and maybe that should have made me feel better. It hadn't. It had only made it harder to keep myself from running to him.

"You are courting darkness." Ovide bowed his head and sighed. "It will not do you any good."

I rocked Mia in my arms and nodded toward the kitchen. "Come on. I'll fix you some tea or coffee or whatever you'd prefer. I think there's some cake left, too."

He looked as though he might refuse, but then changed his mind, nodded, and followed me inside. Without thinking, I handed Mia off to him while I shuffled around searching for tea bags, coffee pods, and cake plates.

"With the way y'all gossip, I'm assuming you've heard my story. So, you should already know that I don't *court* darkness. Darkness and I got hitched long ago. We're an old married couple."

I turned to catch Ovide awkwardly holding Mia out in front of him, looking completely out of his element. "I've heard. Do you think she wants something, perhaps? What does she want? Why is she staring at me this way?"

"She's fine. She just likes to study people."

He settled her a little closer to his chest and sighed. "I have been a friend of darkness for centuries."

I leaned against the counter. "Centuries?"

He nodded at me. "We are hundreds of years old. All of us. I am older than the others by several hundred years. I have seen many things."

"And been a friend of darkness the whole time?"

Ovide was looking more comfortable with Mia by the second. He stroked the softness of her little cheek with his fingertip. "Not the whole time. There was happiness for a while. I...I had a mate once."

My heart ached at the word. I had so many questions about what exactly a mate was to them, but I didn't want Ovide to stop talking. I got the feeling that it wasn't very often that he opened himself up enough to share. "You had a mate?"

He nodded. "A long, long time ago, when I was just a boy. I met her in the gardens of my father's castle. She was a beautiful girl. Soft spoken, with a sweet, gentle kindness. Fate led us to each another very early."

"Sky said that mates are together forever." When I realized I was clutching the shirt at my neck, I forced myself to let go. "What happened?"

He stood suddenly and held Mia out to me. "She died."

I stayed where I was, stunned. "That's...that's awful, Ovide."

He nodded. "It was long before I met any of the others, before the hunt began. None of them know. They are all waiting, expecting that I will find a mate here."

"Why...why don't you tell them?"

Ovide just shook his head in response. I stepped forward and took Mia from him as he gently handed her over. "I must go."

"Wait, Ovide. You don't have to leave. You can stay and hang out with us if you want. Have some cake." I felt like maybe he needed someone to be...a friend.

"I do not think Armand would appreciate me hanging out with his mate."

"Yeah, well, I think that's irrelevant. Did you miss the gossip about him hitting the town and getting up close and personal with bar floozies?"

He blew out a big breath. "I did not miss the gossip. It is not as it seems. Armand has never desired to get 'close and personal' with any female but you. This I know. You should talk to him and believe what he tells you. He will not lie to you."

I couldn't find the words to respond. I wanted to believe Ovide. I really wanted to. And the truth was, the thing that was keeping me away from Armand was not what happened at the bar. It was what might happen if my death curse descends on him. I couldn't bear if Armand...

"You have lost much, too, have you not?"

"Everything." I held Mia closer. "Almost everything."

I pressed a kiss to Mia's head. "I didn't think that I could have this, a precious daughter, but I can't let her go. She's mine, and I love her more than anyone ever could love anyone else—more than that even." I blinked away tears. "I will protect her with my life. Nothing will happen to her."

He nodded. "You are right about that. She now has a family of dragons who will allow no harm to befall her."

Something about that thought eased the tightness in my chest. Knowing that the dragons would protect Mia as though she was one of their own was comforting.

"Armand's coming, you know."

I sucked in a breath. "I'm not ready."

He took Mia back from me and, this time, held her easier. "Well, I suggest you get ready quickly. He will not stop—mates are like that."

"But he..."

"For a chance with my mate, I would have gone to hell and back." Ovide looked away. "I tried."

Tears for him filled my eyes. "Oh, Ovide."

"Armand will not give up now that he knows you are his. If you shun him, he will come back and will keep coming back. He chose you even when he thought that there was no way you could be his mate. Even when he knew that, by choosing you, he was sacrificing his life. He did not care about anything but you. And Mia. That's something."

"But—"

"Perhaps you should appreciate that fate has given you something that not many people get."

I clenched his arm. "What if it happens? What if something happens to him? What if I kill him?"

Like an instant big brother, Ovide ruffled my hair. "What if nothing happens? What if you grow old with a dragon mate and your young?"

"I'm so afraid of having to watch him die." I felt panicky, knowing that I was going to have to give Armand an answer. I didn't know what to do—what to say. I knew what my heart wanted, but...

"We are dragons, Angel. It takes a lot more than some puny curse to kill us off."

I watched as he backed away and felt my heart race. "But what if—"

"Do not ask *me* these questions, Angel." He blinked away the emotion in his eyes and rocked Mia back and forth. "I will watch over the youngling while you and your mate talk."

"The nursery is upstairs. Third door on the left. Should I call over a nanny?"

He hesitated. "We're okay...I think."

"I'll call her over. Just in case."

He nodded and then turned, and I watched as he ascended the stairs in my fuzzy pink bathrobe.

Chapter Twenty-Four
ANGEL

I'd learned so much about dragons in the few days since finding out they existed. Spending the day watching huge colorful dragons roll and tumble and mock battle in the sky, then give Nick and Casey rides over the bayou had taken some of the newness out of the initial shock. Still, my mouth fell open when I saw Armand's massive royal-purple dragon shoot like a rocket over the wall of my house and make a precision landing on my lawn. He was the most beautiful of all the dragons I'd seen by far, and my heart fluttered at the sheer magnificence of him.

Standing in my living room, I watched through the picture window as the massive creature perched in my yard, looking in at me. Even if I hadn't seen him before, I would've known it was Armand because of his coloring—the same purple as his eyes.

The dragon looked so sad, mournful even, that I could not stop myself from walking out to him. I stopped just a few feet shy of his large snout and crossed my arms over my chest.

The moment I stopped walking, he shifted back into his human self. And, suddenly, there he was, naked. "I am so very sorry."

"Oh, hell, Armand. This isn't all your fault."

His head hung low, and he dropped to his knees in front of me. "It is my fault. I should have known you were my mate regardless of any other circumstance. Ovide once said that when I met my mate, I would just know. And I did. I should have trusted my instincts."

"I was just mad because, well, I didn't like seeing another woman with her dirty mitts all over you. I didn't like that at all. And, Sky told me you were going to end our little rendezvous, but you never said anything to me about it yourself. That hurt. "

"That is because I was not going to end it. Angel, before you, I tried to find my mate. I was just...going through the motions. But, after I met you, it was as though my world came alive, everything was brighter, more beautiful, more vital. But all the beauty in my life revolved around you—and Mia. There has never been another who has captured my heart as you have."

He ran his hands through his hair, but he remained kneeling with his eyes on the grass. "I came here every night to be with you, not merely for sex but because you and Mia hold my heart. There is no other place I would rather be. Even before you allowed me into your bed, I watched over you both every night."

A sudden realization dawned. "Wait a second. The giant bird that the groundskeepers kept talking about. That wasn't a bird, was it? Or a plane. It was a dragon. It was you."

I dropped to my knees in front of him and grasped his face in my hands, raising it so that I could look into his eyes. How could I not want this man in my life? Then again, how could I?

"I have this black cloud over me, Armand. People around me die. None of you seem to get that."

He had the nerve to actually smile. "Did you see what I was a few moments ago?"

"What?"

"I was a huge fire-breathing dragon. I have lived for hundreds of years. I have survived being hunted by slayers of my kind. I have survived traversing dimensions. I have survived the adaptation to a new world. Why? Because I am a dragon! The idea that your black cloud could pose a threat to me is laughable."

"You're being ridiculous."

"Shall I prove it? Shoot me. Run me off a cliff. Do your best. Nothing you could do to me would hurt me. Dragons are, as humans say, badass. I am not going to die. Neither are you. Neither is Mia." He pulled me into his arms and I went. "Even if any of what you say about a curse is true, your curse has met its match."

Hope surged in my chest. I tried not to get my expectations up too much, but it was hard. "Are you sure?"

"I am safe with you, Angel. More importantly, you are safe with me. Mia is safe with me." He brushed my hair out of my face and smiled softly down at me. "From the moment I saw you, I didn't understand it, but it was as though from that moment, you've branded my heart with your claiming mark."

"How do I know that you're not going to run out?" I was grasping at straws, I knew it, scared to death that there wouldn't be any left to keep me on solid ground.

"Sky and the others, they told you about mates?" When I nodded, he leaned forward and nuzzled his nose over my neck. "They told you about how the claiming mark works? How we will connect on another level, a magical level. We will be bound together for eternity. With dragons, there is no such thing as walking out on your mate. I would have to be dead to not come home to you."

"Oh, Jesus, don't say stuff like that! It's triggering."

He nuzzled my neck again. "I am ready to claim my mate, Angel. Are you ready?"

"I don't know if I'll ever truly believe deep down that you're safe from my curse, but yes, I do want to be your mate."

He sighed. "Did the others tell you that an eclipse is coming? The first in two thousand years."

"No. What kind of eclipse only happens every two thousand years? I've never heard of anything like that."

"It will happen when our home planet, Wyvern, eclipses the light of your star."

"The sun?"

"Yes. When that occurs, the minds of adult unmated male dragons are affected. They do not survive it. Any unmated dragon will descend into swift and certain insanity. Angel, you are more than a mate. You are my good luck charm. You have saved me from certain insanity and death. You are not my curse; you are my salvation."

As he scooped me up in his arms and headed inside toward the bedroom, his words settled in my mind. For the first time since I was a young girl, I felt truly at ease with who I was.

Then, clear as though he spoke aloud, I heard Armand's voice in my head. "Perhaps now we will retire the label Angel of Death and replace it with Angel of Mercy."

The End.

NEXT BOOK IN THIS SERIES...

Ovide lost his mate years ago. Now, he's just biding time until his own demise which, thankfully, will come soon. The eclipse leading him into a slow descent into sweet oblivion is just around the corner.

Margo has never found a man that was worth the risk of heartbreak. No problem, because her smart mouth and sharp tongue scare away even the most persistent suitors.

When an accidentally-on-purpose claiming mark links them for all of eternity, both will have to rethink their plans for the future. But with the protective walls these two have constructed around their hearts, can they even expect to have a future?

P.O.L.A.R.

(**P**rivate **O**ps: **L**eague **A**rctic **R**escue) is a specialized, private operations task force—a maritime unit of polar bear shifters. Part of a world-wide, clandestine army comprised of the best of the best shifters, P.O.L.A.R.'s home base is Siberia...until the team pisses somebody off and gets re-assigned to Sunkissed Key, Florida and these arctic shifters suddenly find themselves surrounded by sun, sand, flip-flops and palm trees.

1. Rescue Bear
2. Hero Bear
3. Covert Bear
4. Tactical Bear
5. Royal Bear

———

BEARS OF BURDEN

In the southwestern town of Burden, Texas, good ol' bears Hawthorne, Wyatt, Hutch, Sterling, and Sam, and Matt are livin' easy. Beer flows freely, and pretty women are abundant. The last thing the shifters of Burden are thinking about is finding a mate or settling down. But, fate has its own plan...

1. Thorn
2. Wyatt
3. Hutch
4. Sterling
5. Sam
6. Matt

———

SHIFTERS OF HELL'S CORNER

In the late 1800's, on a homestead in New Mexico, a female shifter named Helen Cartwright, widowed under mysterious circumstances, knew there was power in the feminine bonds of sisterhood. She provided an oasis for those like herself, women who had been dealt the short end of the stick. Like magic, women have flocked to the tiny town of Helen's Corner ever since. Although, nowadays, some call the town by another name, **Hell's Crazy Corner.**

1. Wolf Boss
2. Wolf Detective
3. Wolf Soldier
4. Bear Outlaw
5. Wolf Purebred

———

DRAGONS OF THE BAYOU

Something's lurking in the swamplands of the Deep South. Massive creatures exiled from their home. For each, his only salvation is to find his one true mate.

1. Fire Breathing Beast
2. Fire Breathing Cezar
3. Fire Breathing Blaise
4. Fire Breathing Remy
5. Fire Breathing Armand
6. Fire Breathing Ovide

———

RANCHER BEARS

When the patriarch of the Long family dies, he leaves a will that has each of his five son's scrambling to find a mate. Underneath it all, they find that family is what matters most.

1. Rancher Bear's Baby
2. Rancher Bear's Mail Order Mate
3. Rancher Bear's Surprise Package
4. Rancher Bear's Secret
5. Rancher Bear's Desire
6. Rancher Bears' Merry Christmas

Rancher Bears Complete Box Set

———

KODIAK ISLAND SHIFTERS

On Port Ursa in Kodiak Island Alaska, the Sterling brothers are kind of a big deal.
They own a nationwide chain of outfitter retail stores that they grew from their father's little backwoods camping supply shop.
The only thing missing from the hot bear shifters' lives are mates! But, not for long...

1. Billionaire Bear's Bride (COLTON)
2. The Bear's Flamingo Bride (WYATT)
3. Military Bear's Mate (TUCKER)

———

SHIFTERS OF DENVER

Nathan: Billionaire Bear- A matchmaker meets her match.
Byron: Heartbreaker Bear- A sexy heartbreaker with eyes for just one woman.
Xavier: Bad Bear - She's a good girl. He's a bad bear.

1. Nathan: Billionaire Bear
2. Byron: Heartbreaker Bear
3. Xavier: Bad Bear

Shifters of Denver Complete Box Set

Printed in Great Britain
by Amazon

When Armand meets Angel, he knows she's not his mate.
She can't be—she's pregnant with another male's child.
Yet, no female has ever claimed his heart as she has.

Angel of Death is cursed.
Everyone around her dies.
The trick, she's learned, is to never get close to anyone.
Damned if she hasn't screwed that up, and her screwup
may endanger the lives of the two people she cares for
the most—the man she's trying desperately not to fall in
love with, and her own newborn daughter.

Armand is willing to give up eternal life to spend what
little time he has left with Angel.
The only problem is, if he dies, Angel will take the blame.

ISBN 9781660690916

90000

9 781660 690916

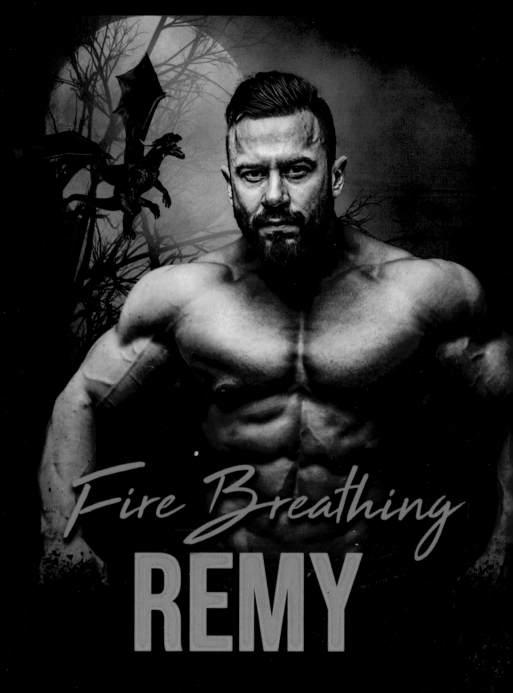

Fire Breathing
REMY
Dragons of the Bayou
CANDACE AYERS